# ARTIFACT

D1560011

## Mark T. Holmes

Also by Mark T. Holmes:

*Streams to Ford – A Poet Revealed*
*Always Ready – Coast Guard Sea Stories from the 1970's*

Cover art courtesy of Tony Pierleoni
www.photosbytp.com

# DEDICATION

My father, Henry T. Holmes, Jr. was a B-24 pilot with the 392nd Bomb Group, 577th Squadron, the unit featured in this book. His missions served as the inspiration for this story and the mission log entries are from his log book with minor tweaks. The content of the missions and events portrayed however are fictional.

I am and always have been in awe of the bravery and skill demonstrated by such young pilots and crew members, thrust into a horrific war, doing things that may have seemed improbable if not impossible, but doing them anyway.

My dad died at an early age, just fifty-eight years old and I truly believe the war shortened his life significantly. How could it not? The fact that he died peacefully in his sleep was a blessing that he truly earned. A few of his traits and experiences plus actual historical events are meshed into this story but overall, it is a fabrication of my imagination.

To my dad and all those who served and fought in the terrible conflict known as the Second World War, I salute you reverently, with deep appreciation for what you accomplished and the sacrifices you made.

# ACKNOWLEDGEMENTS

I am truly appreciative for the opportunity to create this story, inspired by actual missions of the 8th Air Force in World War II. The research portion taught me a lot about the war I did not know, and opened my eyes to the truth behind what actually happened between the United States, Great Britain and the Soviet Union in the run-up to the Cold War.

I must give thanks to the folks who operate the web site B24.net, a source of mission information for my father's unit, with a wealth of insight into mission protocol, crew loading, and other details that were helpful to the creation of this book. Please support this web site and consider joining the 392nd Bomb Group Association.

I appreciate the insight and input from members of the Facebook site "B24 Liberator Fans" for their expertise and feedback and to my son Steve, for reading, advising and offering suggestions for improvements.

*Ukraine gained independence in 1991 and is rightfully and respectfully known today simply as Ukraine although it was commonly referred to as "the Ukraine" during the time of this story. Even though it is slightly out of context to the era, in deference to sensitivities surrounding the former use of the name, I have elected to use the modern version in this story.*

# Chapter One

Gene Jordan was not much taller than a jockey, but he was stoutly built with noticeable forearms, broad shoulders and clear blue eyes that seemed to burn though whatever he set his gaze upon. Even at eighty-nine years old, he commanded a room in spite of his diminutive size, no doubt because of his erect posture, flowing brown hair and gleaming smile. Almost every woman who saw him did a double-take, not quite sure why their blood ran warm in his presence, but found themselves unconcerned with the reason all the same. Did he drink from the fountain of youth and if so, where were those precious waters?

His presence did not go unnoticed by Dolores, the front-of-store manager and co-owner at the Cooper City Antique Mall. Always on the lookout for interesting objects that related to his service in World War II, Gene scoured antique stores up and down the east coast of Florida looking for aviator's wings, insignia, medals, flight logs, jackets, and almost anything connected to the Army Air Corps.

Having given up his own car several years ago, Gene was a frequent Uber user, taking delight in meeting different people, riding in their assorted cars and skirting the high-priced cabs he used to take. Over time, he'd settled on one or two drivers for most of his outings. Even with all his trips, it was still cheaper and vastly safer than driving himself.

Gene's World War II collection included leather pilot helmets, .50 caliber shell casings, 8th Air Force patches, and of course, his own staff sergeant stripes. Oddly enough, he'd also kept the leather leash he used to walk his dog when he was not busy flying with his old crew in the 392nd Bomb Group back in England. He missed them all, and they were all dead and gone. All except for him.

Henry Thomas, the shop owner appeared from the back room with a curious look, spying the old gentleman wandering through his store.

"May I be of service?" Henry inquired with a tone much more formal than Gene was used to hearing in South Florida, where you'd be lucky to have a disinterested clerk look up from his or her smartphone long enough to acknowledge your presence.

"Why yes," replied Gene. "Do you happen to have any artifacts from World War II?"

"We have a few. Most of them are in a showcase near the front of the store. Please come with me."

Leading the way, Henry Thomas made small talk with the elderly visitor, asking about his interests in collecting, secretly hoping to get a lead on some quality estate items should this old gentleman be of the mind to sell at some point in the near future.

It was always like that – constantly searching for inventory. It became a mindset, and a seven-days-a-week obsession to uncover treasures great and small to present to his eager customers. Henry and his wife Shelby were constantly attending estate sales, garage sales, auctions and flea markets in the pursuit of old and vintage items that could be bought for reasonable prices with enough room to mark them up to make a decent profit.

"Here we go," said Henry, pointing to a locked Lucite case that held a number of smalls – industry lingo for small collectible items. "Do you see anything that interests you?"

The old man studied the case, his clear eyes jumping from one item to the next. There was an old pair of aviator sunglasses, not dissimilar from the ones he wore back in 1944. He saw several sets of lieutenant bars, a colonel's oak leaf rank, a few 8th and 9th Air Force patches and assorted medals of no particular value.

"Let me see that old flight log if you please."

"Of course," replied Henry, unlocking the case and extracting the small, two by four inch book along with an acorn-size piece of metal. The book had no markings on it and the inside contained brief notes about some missions flown but no identifying unit information or names. The only details that indicated it was from World War II were the dates and unmistakable target names such as Kiel, Beveland, Hamburg, Hanover and the name that stuck out to Gene the most, Cologne.

"The book and this piece of metal came in together, so I'm selling them as a lot," Henry Thomas explained.

He flipped through the booklet and hefted the odd piece of metal in his hand, gauging its weight. Then his eyes grew wide and he took a half-step back, nearly tripping over his own feet, letting out a muffled sound.

He gasped. "Oh, my God!"

"What is it?" Henry was concerned the old man would fall over and sue him, or keel over from a heart attack. It wouldn't be the first time he'd been victim of a slip-and-fall trick or had to call an ambulance. He reached out to steady the man by grasping his arm, and noticed the strength with which Gene held on.

Henry pulled up a classic Windsor armchair from a nearby booth and insisted the shaken customer take a seat. He trotted over to the kitchen to fetch the old man a cup of cold water.

"Tell me, what is it?" Henry was confused and concerned, but mostly didn't want an incident in his store.

"It's nothing, really," insisted the old man but the beads of sweat emerging from his forehead and the man's suddenly unsteady voice told Henry something else. He waited for the man to speak again, not wanting to push the issue.

"Well, I can hardly believe it." Gene rolled the tarnished piece of shrapnel in his right hand, remembering how he had first picked up the hot metal from the flight deck of the old B-24 so many years ago. The handwriting in the book was familiar to him also. It was the distinctive printing style of his old ship commander, Lieutenant Fred Forshay, or as he insisted on being called, "Freddie."

A chill ran down the old man's spine as he recalled the entire incident as if it were playing out on a wide screen right in front of him, complete with the loud barking of his own twin .50 caliber Browning machine guns and the thumping sounds that erupted from nearby flak bursts. He gulped down the water while he decided whether or not to reveal his long-kept secret to this antique store dealer.

# Chapter Two

*Over Exposure* was a sturdy old bird, and she had a lucky crew, unscathed through eighteen missions over Germany. On today's mission however, it seemed as if every German gunner was intent on ruining that streak of good luck as unrelenting flak exploded around the plane while it made its final approach to the heavily defended marshalling yards near Karlsruhe. Lieutenant "Freddie" Forshay had just made the final turn along with the rest of the B-24's from the 577th Squadron of the 392nd Bomb Group.

It took steady nerves and a willful determination not to yank the controls back from the bombsight-interfaced autopilot as the bomber sheared its way through the barrage of exploding bits of rock and metal. No one in the crew ever got used to it. They just held on for dear life, as they had done so many times before even while watching other ships take direct hits and plunge from the clouds to the oddly and randomly shaped fields spread out far below.

Maddy Schweitzer often wondered what it would be like to fall from the sky, plane parts and other crew members falling with him, returning the hard way to his parent's homeland. A year older than Fred, he'd grown up in the Bronx as

Meinhard Schweitzer but none of the neighborhood kids liked saying his name so they simply called him Maddy. When the country was drawn into war, he insisted on using the nickname instead of his German-sounding given name. As the *Over Exposure* co-pilot his idle thoughts rarely lasted more than a moment, and in this particular moment he yelled over to Freddie to put on his damned helmet.

Freddie Forshay sported a clipped moustache that framed a bright smile and he had a confidence that was infectious; thoroughly unexpected from a young, twenty-two-year-old pilot. They were all young, some as young as eighteen, and the old man of the crew, Gus Fletcher was just thirty-one.

Gus was the flight engineer, and a good one, who kept an eye on all the instruments and made patchwork, in-flight repairs the best he could to keep the heavy bird in the air as it suffered through puffs of German flak and bullets from marauding German ME-109s and FW-190 fighters. He was an avid photographer and camera collector, the proud owner of an Argus C3 "brick" camera. In fact, the aircraft name *Over Exposure* came from Gus, with artwork featuring an exposed female hiding behind a film strip. The name also reflected the crew's feelings about being exposed to flak and fighters.

Since there were no fighters over the target area today and none likely, Freddie exercised his discretion as commander and called the ball turret gunner up from his squatting position in the glass-encased turret hanging below the lumbering B-24. No need to directly expose Gene to more flak than necessary. Gene Jordan was a tough little SOB, and in spite of his short stature and young age had a strict policy of not taking shit from anyone, officer or enlisted. He scrambled along the narrow catwalk in the bomb bay and with nothing to do other than call out oxygen checks, Gene plopped down next to Technical Sergeant Withers, the radio operator. Why not put some equipment between the flak bursts and the flesh and besides, he could certify the bomb drop from here just as easily as from his turret.

Freddie eschewed wearing the leather helmet, figuring the rather thin layer of material between his head and any stray bullets or flak fragments would do no good anyway. He didn't sweat the flak much; if it was going to kill him, so be it. He'd already become tough as nails years earlier at the heel and belt of his father.

Growing up in little Georgetown Connecticut, Fred Forshay was the oldest of eight children, born to a scowling French father and winsome Finnish mother, both immigrants as young children, settling in Connecticut after briefly living in Brooklyn. They met and married young, and Fred was their first child, born in the spring of 1922 on a warm, sunny day.

Jack Forshay was mostly uneducated, a plumber by trade and a master disciplinarian, especially to his oldest son. By the second generation, ushered in with the birth of Fred, the Faucheux name, Americanized to Forshay at Ellis Island back in 1903, was already lost to history. Young Jacques Faucheux had become Jack Forshay by the pen of a surly immigration clerk. It mattered not to Fred who was not a rebellious sort but he didn't have to be – his father found fault in him for the slightest reason, and took out his own demons on Fred almost daily at the end of a belt strap.

Fathering eight children, Jack found it impossible to make ends meet on his salary and so after attending nearby Henry Abbott Technical High School for only a couple of years, Fred was forced to quit school and became a laborer to help pay some family bills.

An excellent student, it was an indignity that burned deeper and hurt more than any physical punishment his odious father ever dispensed. However, Fred rose to the need, mindful of his seven siblings who needed food and clothing. He worked long and hard to supplement the family income, concealing a smirk as he thought about his father who was unable or maybe unwilling to fully provide for his family through his efforts alone.

With that toughness embedded, Freddie was not as interested in protecting his noggin as "Mother" – Fred's endearing term for Maddy, but he relented to his co-pilot's whining voice and doffed his uniform cap, replacing it with the tight-fitting leather helmet.

Anti-aircraft fire was moderate but accurate on the bomb run and almost immediately, flak exploded quite near and slightly above the left wing of the plane, shooting hot metal shards in all directions, including towards the cockpit of *Over Exposure*. The sound was instantaneous with the burst, and to his horror, Maddy saw Fred's head snap to the right. He thought the worst.

It was like being smacked with a ball-peen hammer, Fred recalled, thinking about the piece of hot metal that struck a glancing blow to his helmeted head and bounced to the cockpit deck. It was painful and it nearly knocked him unconscious, but he'd felt the same if not worse at the end of his father's belt.

"Jordan, get up here with the first aid kit – now!" Maddy shouted over the interphone. Gene grabbed the kit and lurched the few feet forward and up to the cockpit, but Lieutenant Fred was already shaking it off and there was no blood. The sergeant eyed the horrified face of the co-pilot while Freddie tried to overcome the sharp pain. The young sergeant picked up an acorn-sized piece of metal from the deck with his gloved hand.

"Here's a souvenir for you, Captain!" Gene referred to his Lieutenant as "Captain" as in the captain of a ship. Fred managed a half-smile through the intense pain and reached back with his right hand, pointing to a small gap between the tubular frame and the back of the pilot's seat. Gene tucked the still-hot metal in its place for safe-keeping.

"I think you saved my life, Mother." Fred eventually smiled weakly as the flak continued to explode around them. Maddy just shook his head slowly, back and forth, relieved that his pilot and friend was still with him.

The twenty bombers in the attack group dropped two hundred twenty-four bombs through the overcast sky, ostensibly on target, but results were barely visible through the cloud cover. Returning to Wendling, the nine-hour mission was a tough one with seven B-24's seriously damaged by flak resulting in the need for nine engine changes.

Fred, Maddy and navigator George Feinstein along with bombardier Robert Roberts headed off to their small Quonset hut to rack out, the pain in Freddie's head still throbbing, but not enough to warrant a visit to the infirmary.

Maddy would have insisted on it, but he knew Fred would rather bunk with the cooks than see an Army doctor.

The little hut, also known locally as a Nissen hut housed the four officers of *Over Exposure* in what can only be called basic living conditions. The hut mostly kept them dry and a small wood stove offered some meagre warmth. For sport, and much to the displeasure of their commanding officer, the officers would fire their sidearms at the rats who routinely invaded their space. The hut offered a bed to sleep in, something that could not be said for the dog-faces pounding through the hedgerows a few hundred miles away in France.

Fred tossed his flight log into his foot locker along with the little metal souvenir from today's mission. He vowed to carry that hunk of shrapnel as a reminder of the day he was nearly killed, if indeed he survived the next few missions at all. In fact, the lucky shrapnel piece rode with Fred the next ten missions or so as he and the crew continued their streak of good luck, even as *Over Exposure* received more damage from flak and fighters as the missions piled up, summer into fall.

# Chapter Three

Slowly, the haze lifted from Fred Forshay's vision, as he glanced around the strange room, not sure where he was, or what had happened the night before. His head was throbbing, the result of excessive celebrating during the three-day layoff from flying. Inclement weather was bad for flying, but good for enjoying some down time.

The weather was still foggy and grey, like his mood. The warmth of his companion however was comforting and newly familiar, the gentle curve of her lower back an inviting spot to rest his free hand, while reaching for a cigarette with his other.

Patricia Prentiss was vibrant and intelligent, something Freddie admired, and she was a reminder of exactly what Freddie and his mates were fighting for – the comfort of a loving woman, the warmth of an open hearth and the freedom to enjoy a glass of beer.

Beyond that, the politics of it all didn't matter to Fred; he was more pragmatic, a follower of his own instincts rather than any one ideology. Frankly, he enjoyed the hell out of flying and vowed to continue a career in the air if he made it through the hellish war. The fact that his job involved dropping bombs on people didn't trouble him much. They were the enemy and they needed to be stopped. There was no confusion or hesitancy, not on his part.

Patty was a few years older than Fred, educated at St. Hugh's at Oxford, one of the first women's colleges associated to the legendary school back in 1886. She was a brilliant linguist, something that was God-given, and spoke fluent Russian as well as French, German and of course, Spanish.

With the cover of working as an administrator at the nearby hospital, a makeshift but professional operation, Patty was also working for the Secret Intelligence Service MI5 division, feeding false information to the Germans, and was on call for assisting with translation needs for assorted dealings with the Russians. With typical British stoicism, she of course kept those details to herself, not even revealing a hint to her new bedside companion, the handsome Lieutenant Forshay.

Her "chance" meeting a few weeks ago with Freddie at the local *King's Head* pub was no accident, their introduction having been handled by the 392nd's own intelligence officer, Colonel John Reed, and with the cooperation of the pub's owner, the curmudgeonly "Sir" Colin Nichol. While he had earned no awards from the British Empire so far as his customers knew, the title he insisted on gave him a measure of satisfaction.

The Colonel wanted the young pilot he'd selected for a very special operation to have feelings for the British spy, hoping that he'd be extra protective of her when the chips were down. It was a rotten thing to do thinking about it, but war was rotten after all.

Colonel Reed had already determined that the young lieutenant's flying skills and valor would come in handy for a special mission that was in the making. He needn't know about any of the details until the last moment, and after Miss Prentiss had vetted him. Fred was not the only one left in the dark about the full scope and scale of the upcoming assignment. The less known by the fewest number of people, the better for all.

Awake now and alert in more ways than one, Freddie deftly swung up and on top of the dozing Miss Prentiss, arranging himself in tight formation behind her ripe posterior. Just as the young scholar was contemplating a clever counter move to Freddie's opening gambit, the alarm clock clanged its annoying alert.

"Freddie darling, I really have to get going, but if you'll keep that dirty little thought of yours in mind, maybe we can examine it in detail some other time."

Sighing and heaving an impatient sound, Lieutenant Forshay collapsed to the bed next to Patricia, feigning disappointment while knowing all the while that he too had to get dressed and back to base. Colonel Reed had set him up for an appointment at 0900 and it was never wise to be late for a meeting with the group's intelligence leader.

A short bicycle ride away from Miss Prentiss' rented room, the air base at Wendling was strewn across the open, gently rolling landscape of northeastern England. Named for the nearby train station, the base was actually a bit closer to the town of Beeston but both towns equally enjoyed the presence and spending of the American visitors. The airfield itself had a pentagon-shaped outer perimeter encasing three crossing runways leaving a grassy triangle in the middle. The longer main runway was most commonly used to give the lumbering B-24's plenty of ground to assure a safe take-off. The support facilities including the briefing room, living quarters, mission planning offices and other administrative buildings occupied an equally large area immediately to the west of the actual airfield and adjacent to if not engulfed by the village of Beeston.

Freddie rolled up to the briefing room at 0855 with just enough time to straighten his uniform and check himself in the reflection of the smudged window on the building's front door. He knew from experience that showing up five minutes early was expected, and showing up on time meant you were late. A week's worth of sweeping the runway at his advanced flight training school had taught him that lesson after showing up a few moments late for just one pre-flight briefing.

Colonel Reed accepted the young lieutenant's crisp salute and asked him to have a seat.

"Lieutenant Forshay, you've completed twenty-eight missions without a casualty, you've observed flight discipline with the best of my officers, and word has it, you're sharp as a tack."

"I'm always eager to learn, sir," replied the slightly nervous pilot.

"Can I have your commitment that what you're about to hear is to be held in the strictest confidence, lieutenant?"

"Yes sir, of course."

The colonel looked through the window of the office and nodded to the adjutant watching from the hall. With that, a tall British officer briskly strode down the hall and entered the briefing room.

"Colonel Melkin, meet Lieutenant Forshay of the 577th Squadron."

Freddie smartly stood and saluted the senior officer, and grasped his outstretched hand, nodding his head in a formal way.

"Pleased to meet you, sir."

"Forshay is it? That's a French name."

"Yes sir, but with an American spelling."

"Ah yes," the Colonel replied, pulling on his chin. "The handiwork of an overzealous immigration officer I should imagine."

"Yes sir, when my father came to America, they were rather clumsy in coming up with surnames they could easily spell."

"Well, enough small talk then. Colonel, does he know?"

Colonel Reed said nothing but shook his head. No way was he going to spill the beans before the SIS officer met his recommended pilot for such a weighty mission.

"Good." Colonel Melkin reached into his haversack and pulled out a manila folder marked "Top Secret" and placed it in front of the lieutenant. To emphasize the moment, he lit one of his American cigarettes and dragged on it deeply then leaned forward, his face just inches from the lieutenant.

"What do you know about Operation Frantic?"

Not only did Freddie not know anything about any Operation Frantic, it sounded like a name made up by some pointy-headed desk jockey back in Washington.

"Never heard of it, sir." Colonel Melkin glared at him for a long moment, taking measure of the lieutenant's response. He believed him.

"Good. What you learn of it today shall not leave this room, understood?"

"Yes sir, my lips are sealed."

"Excellent. Colonel, will you brief him?"

Colonel Reed opened the manila folder marked "Top Secret" and began shuffling through the pages within, taking out and unfolding a detailed map of Eastern Europe. It was unfamiliar to Freddie, as the maps used for their missions seldom showed anything beyond the actual target areas in Germany.

"Son, we're asking you to volunteer for a special mission that could have implications far beyond the war we're currently engaged in, possibly affecting the makeup of Europe and even the United States for many years to come."

"We need you to fly a mission to Ukraine to deliver a package of the highest value and return safely. It will require you to simulate combat damage in flight and withdraw from the formation before proceeding on to your destination. That's about all we can tell you right now. You'll be fully briefed as the mission date approaches."

Freddie gulped. Twenty-eight

missions in the books and just seven more before a ticket home, and they had to pick me to save the world? How did a twenty-two-year-old kid from Connecticut get caught up in such a situation? He sighed deeply and thought for a minute.

Being asked to volunteer was just a polite way to say you've been picked for a job. No need to pretend otherwise, still he felt the urge to formally reply.

"Of course, sir, whatever you need. I'm your man."

# Chapter Four

Gene Jordan finished the cup of water so graciously provided by Henry Thomas. It was just what he needed to overcome the shock of seeing that rough piece of shrapnel he last held in his hand seventy-one years go.

Collecting himself, he sat upright in the old chair, looked wistfully at his host, and offered a slight smile reflecting on the flashback he'd just experienced. While he certainly had never expected to stumble upon any relics from his own squadron much less his very own crew, the sight of the log book and piece of shrapnel snapped his mind to attention, thinking back to those heady summer and fall days back in England.

Only eighteen years old then, Gene had aced gunner's school, finishing second in his class, exhibiting a flair for accurate shooting at moving objects thanks to the many times he'd gone duck hunting with his uncle Jeremy.

His skills were quickly evident during the five-week course at the old Las Vegas Army Airfield where he advanced rapidly from static firing to truck-mounted shooting and finally shooting at moving targets from a flying bomber. The school was designed for flexible training, enabling a gunner to be skilled at shooting from several positions in the aircraft. What made Gene an ideal ball turret gunner was his diminutive size.

Barely five feet, five inches tall, the young Mr. Jordan was an automatic fit for the confined space of the cramped ball turret hanging beneath the plane. It was an achingly awkward position within that ball, sitting in kind of a fetal position tucked into the small space along with two heavy machine guns, sights and ammo. The Sperry ball turret was small to reduce drag and so the smallest gunner in the crew was assigned to it.

Gene often wondered if any of the designers of this little torture chamber had ever spent hours on end inside of it, guns clanging in their ears, freezing half to death in the cold atmosphere while flying above hostile territory.

It didn't matter. Gene Jordan was tough as nails having fought his way through adolescence as the only way to survive the inevitable rash of bullies who routinely picked on him, figuring on an easy target. They were each wrong and sorry for having tried to push around the scrawny kid. Gene knew how to stick up for himself and he was ruthless in his defense, kicking bigger boys in the balls if necessary, scratching their eyes, punching them in the throat. Whatever it took to win the fight, Gene did it, and he came to enjoy the challenge. He didn't carry a chip on his shoulder; it was more like a two by four.

The emotional challenge he faced now however, threatened to overwhelm him in front of strangers, and that wouldn't do. He abruptly stood to his feet, handing the book and metal shard back to Henry Thomas.

"Not interested," he said, and strode out the front door, fighting back tears as he walked.

Mystified, Henry Thomas replaced the items in the Lucite box and affixed the lock, pulling on it to make sure it was closed, wondering exactly what power lay in those small items to cause an old man to nearly pass out, and then rush out of his store without an explanation.

"Have you ever seen him before?" Henry asked Dolores, quizzically.

"No, I think he's a first time visitor," she replied.

"He'll be back," said Henry.

# Chapter Five

No one likes to be roused awake at 0430, especially someone who just got the weight of the world laid at his feet - or so it felt. Mission planners seemed to have no regard for bomber crews' sleep and regardless of the target today, 0430 was simply not acceptable, not to Freddie Forshay or any of his sleepy crew.

Fred had been in the middle of a dream about flight school. Soaring above the clouds in the PT-17 trainer was exhilarating, and if nothing else, an enormous adventure for someone who grew up in fear of his father's demons and the end of his belt. The freedom of flight released his soul, letting the wounds of his youth finally scab over. Flying that nimble biplane was a release from the dark past. No more working on a road crew so his sisters could eat. He was on his own, preparing for the war overseas, but free from the war at home. At last.

After a quick breakfast, crew briefings for twenty-two ships commenced at 0515 and lasted more than an hour. The target was an airfield at Osnabruck with the option to drop bombs on a nearby railroad marshalling yard if the main target was obscured by weather.

Before grabbing a ride out to the flight line, Freddie ran back to his Quonset hut to retrieve his good luck charm, the hunk of shrapnel that nearly killed him a while ago. There had to be a good omen involved. After all, Mother was always needling him about something so the fact he insisted that his pilot don his helmet seconds before the nearly fatal flak burst had to have come with a higher meaning. At least that's how Freddie saw it and he was not one to tempt the fates.

The briefing officer's word of warning about the Nazi's new jet fighter planes echoed in his thoughts as the jeep pulled up to the ship. *Over Exposure* had the few flak holes patched up and Gus had pronounced it fit as a fiddle.

Compared to the more refined looking B-17 Flying Fortress, the B-24 Liberator actually had a longer range, could carry a heavier bomb load, had a higher top speed, and used the advanced Davis wing design, offering better fuel efficiency and allowing for the greater range. The main drawback of the Davis wing was its lesser ability to withstand battle damage. It simply couldn't absorb as much misery as the B-17 and stay in the air.

In spite of the advancements in range and speed, the Liberator had a lower operating ceiling than the graceful B-17 and so was something of an easier target for the generally accurate anti-aircraft guns of the German Army. In fact the B-24 became known as the "widow-maker" - a name not lost of the crew of *Over Exposure* or the other aircrews in the 392nd and other deployed squadrons flying the plane.

Fred was not so absorbed with the flak however. After all, he had beaten it now, and he had his lucky charm. It was the new fighters that occupied his thoughts as he and Maddy ran through their long pre-flight checklist.

The Achmer Airfield near Bramsche in the Osnabruck district had become a test site for the new ME-262 jet fighter, the first turbojet fighter plane to see combat. Led by the daring Walter Notowny, the unit bore his name – Kommando Notowny – the airfield received the advanced unit in September of '44, rushing modifications to completion to handle the new fighters. The potential significance of the jets was not lost on Allied commanders who singled out the airfield for attack.

It had quickly become evident that the only way to effectively duel the ME-262 was to attack it on the ground, while taking off or landing, or while it was in slow maneuvers. Otherwise, the plane could attain almost one hundred miles per hour more in airspeed than the fastest Allied fighters, could keep its speed in tight turns, and was nearly impossible to intercept in high speed maneuvers.

Under Notowny's direction, and through some trial and error, the most effective tactic devised to attack bomber formations was a "roller coaster" maneuver, rising up and behind a bomber group, swooping down through the ineffective fighter escorts if present, and then rising again, slightly behind and below the bombers to make a brief gun attack at a more stable and slightly slower speed of approach.

The ME-262's speed to the target under level or diving flight was such that a mere two seconds of time was available for firing guns on the target. Combining the limited range of its guns and the high rate of speed on approach, there was precious little time to set up and fire. The effects of the 30-millimeter cannons, in spite of the brief firing time could be devastating on the Allied bombers.

Following an extensive seventy-five minute briefing, eight ships from the 577th took off around 0830, along with an additional fourteen planes from the 578th and 579th Squadrons, with *Over Exposure* in the lead; all loaded with a mix of two hundred-fifty and five hundred pound bombs and a determination to knock out Achmer's ME-262 facility.

Tucked into his ball turret as *Over Exposure* crossed the English Channel, Sergeant Jordan wondered aloud how he'd square off against the fast Nazi jets, if they came up to attack.

"You doin' OK, Jordo?" Sergeant Taggert the tail gunner nervously inquired, knowing he'd also be face to face with the new fighters.

"Nothin' to it," replied Jordon, "and don't call me Jordo." He shook his head and let out a quiet profanity. Every stinking flight, Taggert would call him "Jordo" and every stinking flight, he'd tell the tail gunner not to do it. After twenty-eight missions, though, he considered the routine to be another lucky charm, so the admonishment was mild, and met with a muted chuckle by Taggert.

On the flight deck, Lieutenant Forshay and Mother settled on the course provided by Lieutenant Feinstein. They were heading for Osnabruck, located in northwestern Germany, less than fifty miles from the Dutch border and forming the western point of a triangle created by Bremen and Hanover. The remaining B-24's formed up behind *Over Exposure* for the rather short, six-hour mission.

Gus had his Argus C3 35mm camera along for the ride as usual, and from the lead position in the formation, had a chance to take some great photos. On the trip across the English Channel, he scampered back to the waist gunner position and shot an entire roll of film, mostly of nearby B-24's but also portraits of Sergeants Talbot and Lowry though they were nearly unrecognizable in their cold weather gear. In fact, Gus had to keep his camera tucked in his own suit so the film and camera mechanisms didn't freeze.

Would today be a milk run as everyone hoped or something far worse? The answer would soon be evident. Trying hard to focus on today's mission, Freddie couldn't help but wonder about his next mission, the one he'd dare not share with Maddy or anyone else, at least not now.

# Chapter Six

Officially, the British had no real interest in Operation Frantic, Churchill figuring it was not strategically viable, and so declining to throw the support of the United Kingdom behind it. But that didn't mean it wasn't of some value.

The brainchild of the Americans, Operation Frantic had been in the works for a couple of years, offering the notion of shuttle-bombing enemy targets out and back, by having bombers and escorts that had departed England or Italy for their initial bombing runs land at Soviet-hosted air bases in Ukraine, reloading, and returning home while making a second bombing attack. There was also an interest in eventually employing bases in Siberia that could potentially be used to attack Japan.

Operation Frantic also offered an opportunity to build up US-Soviet relations as the war inevitably drew to a close. This was not lost of Stalin, who had refused the plan a number of times before acquiescing early in 1944, when it suited his needs. Access to American technology could be invaluable for the future of the

USSR. He feigned cooperation as a ruse to get American aircraft and the even more valuable and perhaps gullible American soldiers on his home turf.

While Churchill had no desire to try shuttle bombing, he did like the idea of having access to Soviet air bases, facilities and personnel. He assigned a small contingent from SIS to partner with the Americans on potential intelligence opportunities. He had to know what the Russians were capable of, just in case.

Colonel Melkin was the source of the idea Churchill liked most – planting a female spy at one of the bases in Ukraine with access to the leader of the Soviet's local contingent of Operation Frantic, a highly decorated general and probable post-war influencer. Finding a cooperative ally with the ambitious and somewhat reckless Colonel Reed of the 392nd Bomb Group gave Melkin the means to bring his plan to life. A few double vodkas during their first meeting at the old *King's Head* pub helped to draw in the enthusiastic American colonel.

Spending many millions of dollars and overcoming enormous logistics challenges, the United States literally transported every gallon of aviation gas, metal runway section, every tent pole, all the munitions, and everything else needed to build air bases from scratch all the way to Ukraine via ships to Murmansk then by trains the rest of the way. It was a testimony to the unfailing, "get it done" attitude that served the US so well, not only in Europe but in the Pacific too, not to mention the homeland workers who built the many thousands of tanks, planes, ships and other war-essential items. The stunning capabilities of the Americans and what it implied was not lost on Josef Stalin.

The Soviets supplied the locations while the US supplied the cash, men, and materials. Bases were established in Poltava, Mirgorod and Pyriatyn, spread across the vast open flatlands of east-central Ukraine. To the American's dismay, the Soviets insisted on providing base security, a colossal mistake that ensured the almost complete failure of the operation during its brief lifetime.

In spite of the operational shortcomings, the access to Soviet facilities and personnel was unprecedented and eye-opening at the same time. While the cost was high, the potential for US-Soviet post-war cooperation was somewhat justified but the potential intelligence value was the real reason for the effort. Churchill knew it but wouldn't acknowledge it one way or the other, even if he felt some of the Americans were a bit wide-eyed about the whole endeavor. He'd find a way to ride the well-intentioned coattails of the Americans for his own useful purposes.

# Chapter Seven

Gene Jordan's first-floor apartment overlooked the fourth green at Deer Creek Country Club, situated at a distance so that he could watch the chipping and putting without having to hear much of the insipid golf conversations. Not a golfer himself, he still enjoyed the wide expanse of greenery, trees, water features and the afternoon sun that graced the finely kept grounds of his assisted living facility.

Gene Jordan sold the place he and his wife had bought when they first moved to Florida, a new development near the ocean with a great view of both the Atlantic and the nearby inland waterway. After she passed, he elected to live out his remaining years at his new place where cooking, cleaning and all the other chores were taken care of by the staff. Deerfield Beach had a lot to offer seniors, and it was an ideal jumping off point for cruises, airplane travel, and the beach for those still active enough to enjoy the sun and water.

Sitting back in his favorite wicker chair on the expansive, screened in patio, he looked lovingly at a large photo of his deceased wife, and sipped on a cup of Earl Grey tea while mulling over what he had seen at the antique mall. The brief description of each mission in the log book brought back searing memories of his time in the air with Lieutenant Fred and the rest, doing their duty, scared as all hell while doing it.

He thought of his old dog, Spencer, the slightly gimpy but hugely charming English bulldog that had belonged to a buddy of his who didn't return from one particularly heinous mission, and was bequeathed to Gene. It was very formal, with notarized paperwork and all. In turn, Gene had prepared for his own potential demise, assigning Spencer to a sergeant in the ground crew in case of disaster. Spencer had quickly warmed up to Gene, and lustily greeted him each time he returned from the sky. Spencer was also Winston Churchill's middle name. It seemed oddly appropriate.

He didn't need the flight log to remember each mission with his brothers of the sky, and could clearly see each of their faces, as if he had just landed at Wendling, everyone anxious to get debriefed and have some chow. *Over Exposure* had been their steady ride for most of the missions, but they'd swapped planes now and then when *Over Exposure* needed some repairs and TLC. The borrowed B-24's all were named for reasons that meant something to her crews, at least at some point in time: Pregnant Peg II, Little Lulu, Old Standby, Alfred IV, Puss 'N Boots, and one with no name, just number "604" and a painting of a scantily clad young lady. Each one brought them back safely, and for that, Gene and the crew were thoroughly grateful. In the log book, Fred's unmistakable hand noted each mission result with typical pilot brevity:

*Mission #1: July 18, 1944 to Troarns, longitude 0°6' W, latitude 49° 10' N. We bombed guns and German troops. Heavy accurate flak. No fighters. Quite a few flak holes. #3 engine knocked out.*

Gene thought to himself, "What a way to get introduced to the war, bombing right next to Montgomery's flank and being hammered by flak the first time out, plus an ungodly 4:00 a.m. takeoff! Seventeen out of forty-five ships were damaged. There was nothing for me to shoot at, but would every mission be so dangerous?"

*Mission #2: July 19, 1944 to Koblenz,*

*longitude 8° 10' W, latitude 50° 20' N. Bombed marshaling yards. Moderate accurate flak and rockets. A few flak holes.*

The mission was in a new ship while the other one got patched up. Well, Freddie was brief in his description, that's for sure. Two days, two missions. "At this rate," Gene remembered, "We'd be heading home in five weeks!"

*Mission #3: July 24, 1944 to St. Lo, longitude 1° 5' W, latitude 49° 18' N. Provided troop support. Bombed guns and German troops. Heavy accurate flak. A few holes.*

"Well," Gene recalled, "We were now in our regular ship, *Over Exposure*, on another mission with heavy flak. Still nothing for me to shoot at, but plenty scary enough."

It still gave him shivers down his spine seventy years after the fact. Curiously, at the debriefing, all crews were warned not to discuss the mission with anyone.

*Mission #4: July 25, 1944 to St. Lo, longitude 1° 5' W, latitude 49° 18' N. Troop support. Bombed guns and German troops. Heavy accurate flak. Went in at 11,000 feet. Quite a few flak holes.*

Still nothing to shoot at, but plenty of exploding flak on a back-to-back mission to the same damned spot. Bombs were dropped accurately, in concentration.

*Mission #5: July 29, 1944 to Bremen, longitude 8° 50' E, 53° 5' N. We bombed oil refineries and storage tanks. Heavy flak, rockets, and fighters. Lost #3 engine halfway to target. Went in, bombed, and came home on 3 engines. A few flak holes. Saw our element leader get hit and go down in a spin.*

Gene paused, thinking about the toughest mission they'd flow yet. Things were getting into a rhythm – fly a mission, lay low for a few days. He remembered the mission summary declaring there were no fighters.

"The official reports said no fighters, so what was I shooting at?" Twenty-eight planes were flak-damaged. Those damned German gunners were too good, but thankfully, the element leader made it back OK.

*Mission #6: August 3, 1944 to Beveland, longitude 4° 5' E, latitude 51° 28' N. Bombed a bridge as a target of opportunity. Meager flak. No holes.*

Gene closed his eyes and thought back. They had been off duty for a few missions including the one just the day before where Spencer's previous owner Arthur, had been killed in a crash landing.

The target area at Beveland was overcast so the group bombed a bridge in Holland. *Over Exposure* was lucky that day, but even with light flak, one of the ships had to ditch in the English Channel as its crew parachuted to safety. You just never knew.

*Mission #7: August 4, 1944, to Kiel, longitude 10° 8' E, latitude 54° 20' N. Bombed a submarine factory. Heavy, accurate flak, rockets, and fighters. Quite a few flak holes.*

In fact, Gene recalled they'd counted hundreds of holes in the right wing alone after that mission. Nineteen aircraft received battle damage and two men were lost with others injured. This was no longer an adventure. It was certainly not glorious. "It was a hard-core, shitty war," Gene recalled thinking, "And how in the world were we going to survive it?" Battle-weariness was starting to set in. This work was hard on the nerves, even for tough guys.

The afternoon sun was fading now, casting long shadows on the golf course. Carts whizzed by as players wrapped up their rounds of golf and Gene dozed in his chair, the details of the various missions starting to merge into one. The whumping noises of exploding flak echoed in his brain as he fitfully slept.

# Chapter Eight

General Rostislav Kaminsky relaxed on the makeshift portico of his headquarters building, smoking an American cigarette, one of the perks of having so many western guests staying at his current command, the hastily constructed airfield at Poltava. Inside the office that also housed his living quarters, a low groan arose from a poor Russian nurse, the latest victim of Kaminsky's amorous overtures.

Truth be told, while he liked a good romance, he was perfectly satisfied with a simple, if brutal conquest, too. This had been the case an hour earlier, when the curvy Russian nurse resisted his assault. She paid for it dearly, with a black eye, bruised wrists and the humiliation of forced sex. Rostislav or "the vermin" as he was known by a vast sorority of victims, got as much pleasure out of physical assault as he did the ultimate sexual release.

He didn't pretend to understand it, much less care to be redeemed of it. It was war. He was a highly decorated general. Women were chattel, he was their overseer.

Nameless, at least to him, this latest nurse was nothing more than a link in the chain of women he'd conquered over the last two months. Secretaries, nurses, even a few female mechanics – he cared not, and he viewed them all with disdain, not as daughters, mothers and wives. So long as his aides kept bringing them to his quarters, he would keep having his way with them. The privileges of being a decorated general.

Once in a while, one of them would actually respond lustily to the occasion, taking her own pleasure while satisfying the oversexed general. These few escaped the back of his hand and the sting of his leather belt and were invited to return until inevitably he grew tired of the sameness and beat them anyway, simply for the sin of not being someone else.

The abused women were then dispatched to some even more remote and desolate location, adding insult to the infamy of having been one of the vermin's conquests. War was hell for some; worse for others.

Widely considered a legendary airman, and his battle achievements were quite impressive, General Kaminsky was a two-time recipient of the Hero of the Soviet Union, the country's highest award, entitling him not only to the impressive gold star medal, but also a bronze bust that was displayed proudly in his hometown of Vyshelej. He was virtually untouchable by anyone other than Stalin himself. Thus, his offenses against women were simply thought of as innocent peccadilloes, the well-descrved "habit" of a horny, persistent soldier. Although the general's abuse of women was concealed in official channels, word of it reached western shores through various networks.

His "habit" was also his weakness, in the mind of Winston Spencer Churchill, and the indomitable prime minister intended to take advantage of it.

Rostislav Kaminsky was almost embarrassingly polite to his American guests. He wanted them to see him as a pushover, a weak leader who would neither interfere with their operations nor cause them any inconvenience. He'd planned to gain the confidence of the senior American airmen, pump them with alcohol, and find out what they would willingly reveal to him. In most cases, he found little cooperation but all he needed was one or two loose-lipped officers to achieve the advantage.

Any knowledge he could gain would add to his legacy, and keep him in good stead with Josef Stalin, the crazy, ruthless, unrelenting dictator who killed millions of his own people. It was best to put fresh bread on the table from time to time and not count on past successes. He knew it; Stalin expected it.

This Operation Frantic as the allies put it was the perfect opportunity to leverage valuable information and perhaps win a very rare third Hero of the Soviet Union. To win it twice was truly impressive. To win a third would be to join a very select group indeed. Women across the vast Soviet empire would kneel at his feet, both to show respect and more. He was sure of it, and he dreamed of it.

The crazy Americans built Poltava and the two other fields from scratch, using interlocking metal mesh runway sections to cover the hardscrabble ground. They brought in the fuel, the ammunition, tents, and everything else to house and operate an air base in the heart of Ukraine. Leading the Soviet contingent for this foolhardy venture seemed at first like a demotion for a highly decorated general, but Stalin and the Soviet Foreign

Minister Vyacheslav Molotov agreed together that Kaminsky was the right choice to carry out Stalin's will.

Devilishly clever and ruthless, Kaminsky was sure to milk the Americans for every last detail he could get, and pass it along to his superiors. It was exactly what Crazy Joe wanted and expected. After all, he didn't agree to the ridiculous shuttle-bombing plan for its face value. He wanted and needed access to advanced American technology if he was going to beat them and that fat bastard Churchill after he'd finished with the Germans.

# Chapter Nine

Colonel John Reed was livid, but unable to express his frustration or worry to the operations officer of the 392nd Bomb Group. His hand-picked pilot and crew were out on a mission to Germany when he needed them alive and well for his mission to Ukraine. Unable to reveal his needs or his mission, at the risk of a cataclysmic security breach, he stoically waited near the flight line to witness the return of the B-24's even though they were not due for hours.

On *Over Exposure*, it was cold. Real cold. The heavy insulated flight suits helped, as did the somewhat unreliable electric suit heaters but the bitter cold of flying at altitude along with the bulk of the suits, gloves and parachutes made flying combat even more of a challenge. Still, the crew became used to it as best they could.

The unpressurized B-24 required the crew to wear oxygen masks above ten thousand feet or so, adding to the mass and discomfort of their attire. In the 392nd, it was customary to go to oxygen at eight thousand feet especially on shorter missions. It was a lot to manage, but earnest, brave young fliers rose above every obstacle time and again to complete their missions.

Many died doing so, at the hands of expert German pilots and accurate gun crews, and to see your friend's plane go down in flames, well, those feelings were left unspoken. In fact, the 8th Air Force suffered about half of the U.S. Army Air Force's one hundred fifteen thousand casualties during the war including over twenty-six thousand killed.

Gene Jordan took it all in stride. He was going to die someday, and if he died fighting off Messerschmitts or by the chance hit from nearby flak, then so be it. He was going to do his damndest to kill every German pilot he could, and thought nothing of it. *Over Exposure* bombed troops, factories, rail yards and more, and if a few innocents were killed too, that was the cost of war. Those people wanted to kill him, so even-Steven as far as he was concerned.

Living in a black and white world made it simple, not only for Gene but for many of the bomber crews. It was the only way to retain most of your sanity, in a world gone absolutely crazy with war. Live or die. Kill or be killed. There was a certain beauty and peace in the simplicity of it all.

On the flight deck, Fred and Maddy got ready to set up on the IP for Achmer, the initial point and the beginning of the bomb run. Below and forward of them, Lieutenant Feinstein was expertly plotting their position, course and speed, and would soon mark the IP and the start of the terror. So far, there were no fighters of any kind, much less the unknown and therefore dreaded ME-262 jets. George Feinstein was today's lead bombardier of the group's combat box formation – all other ships would drop bombs by his prompt. He had to make sure he was spot-on accurate.

Far below and ahead, the warning claxons sounded at the Achmer airfield. Walter Notowny rallied his pilots into action, determined not to have his precious jets caught on the ground. In the distance the echoes of the outer anti-aircraft gun emplacements could be heard.

Time was not on his side. His plan was to get as many 262's aloft as possible, let the Americans do what they could to the base with their bombs, then pounce on them as they turned for home.

The P-47 Thunderbolt escort

fighters didn't worry him one bit. In spite of being fine aircraft, they would not stop his pilots from bringing hell to the marauding bombers. It would be historic. He would be remembered forever.

Mission reports described the flak as moderate and accurate. The emphasis should have been on accurate with nearly half the Liberators receiving damage heading in to the target. Maddy's mind drifted off once again to falling from the sky, the green farms below racing to meet him, to bring him to his homeland, the only sound being the wind rushing past, the bitter cold slowly giving way to warm air as he approached the hard ground.

A thunderous "whump" as flak exploded ahead to the right with a few shards ripping through the airframe brought Maddy back to reality. Up ahead, the P-47's tried to catch the 262's taking off, but they were a little late to the party. Instinctively, Maddy checked Freddie to see if he was OK. The curled up lip and slight nod assured him all was well and a quick check with the crew on the interphone affirmed the same. Fred checked his jacket pocket to make sure his lucky shrapnel piece was still there.

The God-awful flak was unnerving

and those damned German gunners seemed to get better with every mission, whether cloud cover or clear blue sky.

"We're at the IP," declared George Feinstein. He opened bomb bay doors to signal the other crews. The group was on final approach to the target, under the steady eye of young Lieutenant Feinstein and his advanced Norden bombsight. Noted for its pinpoint accuracy by the manufacturer, in combat practice it seldom lived up to the advertized seventy-five foot circular error probability, but even the twelve hundred foot combat average was acceptable for the technology of the day.

The highly classified Norden bombsight used an analog computer and linkage to the plane's autopilot, allowing for constant adjustments due to wind and speed differences. To get the most out of this advanced bombsight, the ship was at its mercy during the bomb run, regardless of the amount of flak or other terrors the crew might face. The mission came first and the proper use of the Norden gave the best chance for success.

Getting his hands on a Norden bombsight was of the utmost priority for General Rostislav Kaminsky and of course for Josef Stalin. With it, the Soviets could readily copy the technology and build up their own deadly bomber force for the remaining and future war ahead. Little did he know the Americans would virtually hand it to him on a silver platter.

Mostly obscured by cloud cover, the target at Achmer had to be scrapped for the secondary target, nearby marshalling yards at Osnabruck where the skies were more favorable. Feinstein called off the bomb run and quickly arranged for a plot to the nearby marshalling yards. A Pathfinder Force (PFF) led them in, the British Mosquito bombers dropping bright incendiary target indicators over the new target. This alone took some of the pressure off George as the force adjusted to the secondary target and made an accurate drop on the marshalling yards using the PFF flares as the guide.

Somewhat disappointed they hadn't been able to strike the Achmer field, the backup target was still a high value objective and for that, Freddie Forshay was relieved. No one wanted to waste a mission on so-called targets of opportunity. If he was to risk his life and those of his crew, he wanted it to count.

As they were turning for the trip home to Wendling, Sergeant Jordan chimed in on the interphone.

"Captain, I see something coming up fast. I think it's them damned jets."

"Everyone keep your eyes open. You won't have much time," announced Forshay as each gunner snapped to attention, eyes nervously scanning the skies around them.

In the cockpit of the lead ME-262, Oberleutnant Adolf Schuck directed his squadron in the rollercoaster maneuver, diving past the slower Thunderbolts, who gave chase anyway, and then curling up behind the B-24's, slowing the airspeed enough to get a decent two seconds or so of firing on target before having to quickly turn aside.

The pursuing P-47's had no chance of catching Schuck or his fellow pilots as they would quickly accelerate in a climb away from the pesky American fighters.

Each ME-262 pilot selected a bomber to assault and leveling off slightly below and behind the squadron, in the few seconds available fired their MK-108, 30-millimeter cannons with deadly results.

Two of the trailing B-24's erupted into flames as engines caught fire while the tail gunner on each plane was ripped apart by the deadly cannon. Two more, further into the group were also heavily damaged, with engines smoking and devastating damage to the control surfaces. The rudders and most of the elevator surfaces on another B-24 were shot off along with most of the tail turret, as the plane began a slow, descending death spiral. Six parachutes billowed open as the plane continued to fall. Just six.

The ME-262's blasted by the bomber formation, pulling away with a couple hundred yards to spare, screaming upwards, preparing to make a steady turn to the left, and descend down and across the formation again before heading back to base. The lateral approach gave a wider target and the better chance for a kill.

"Here they come!" Lieutenant Robert Roberts shouted his warning from the exposed nose turret of *Over Exposure*. In a flash, the ME-262's blasted down and across the remaining B-24's, cannons ablaze, causing more damage but at high speed, they were only able to get off a quick, one to two-second burst before peeling off and heading back to Achmer. The jets, while fast, were a handful to operate and allowed for only sixty to ninety minutes of total flight time. Two passes through the nearly helpless B-24's would have to do.

A few of the Thunderbolts followed, although at a distance, each pilot knowing that if they could catch the 262's while landing, they'd have a good chance at destroying a few. It would be some measure of payback for the jets wreaking havoc in the bomber formation they were charged with protecting.

In the lead position, *Over Exposure* was not among the primary targets of the flashing Messerschmitts and had escaped largely unscathed. Gene Jordan sat awestruck in his turret, not having had one good shot at any of the marauding German pilots. Even though the closing speed of the jets was slower than he expected, they flashed past quickly, accelerating and climbing at the same time. By the time Lieutenant Roberts saw them pulling away on the first pass, they were already out of gun range.

Oberleutnant Adolf Schuck flew cover while his unscathed jet fighters landed at Achmer, each pilot hastening his approach, knowing that he could be blown apart at any minute during the vulnerable landing. Approaching from behind Schuck's ME-262, Captain Howard Stanley of the U.S. Army Air Corps prepared to register his fifth kill in a month of duty. He'd be an ace, with a jet kill no less, if he could only get a few seconds of quality shooting behind the circling Messerschmitt.

Nosing his Thunderbolt to the right, Stanley and his wingman dove on the jet fighter and opened fire with eight .50 caliber machine guns each, blasting holes through the canopy of the jet, instantly killing one of the Reich's leading aces as he protected his flock. The rest of the attacking P-47's swept across the landing strip, aiming for the parked or taxiing 262's, causing some damage to a few before heading west to escort the remaining B-24's back to the English Channel and the safety of Wendling.

Freddie Forshay heaved a sigh of relief. The jet fighters he'd been warned about were real enough, fast as the devil, and deadly, too. It only took a few hits of 30-millimeter steel case ammo to tear apart a plane. Three bombers were lost plus one more heavily damaged and others beat up as well. In his estimation, it was not a good trade off for having bombed a secondary target. War was war.

"Maddy, take over please." He reached for his thermos of chicken broth to calm his nerves while his mind began pondering the secret mission yet to come. Maddy nodded and hefted the control yoke in his hands, amused at the sudden formality of his flight deck partner and close friend.

Fred thought about the risky mission he'd been briefed on. Although he wasn't told much at this point, he'd have to lead his plane and crew along with his unknown precious cargo, all alone after faking a crash during a regular mission, past Germany to some far-flung airfield in Ukraine. That's where the Russians were. What the hell?

"I'm a twenty-two-year-old kid from Connecticut," reflected Freddie. He rolled his lucky shrapnel piece in his hand. "How in the world did I get myself into this mess?"

At Wendling, it was mid-afternoon, tea time really for the locals and time for the B-24's to come into view, returning from their mission. Colonel Reed waited below the control tower, nervously pulling on his unlit corncob pipe and scanning the horizon for the lumbering planes. As the squadrons came into view, he saw a flare fired from the lead plane. His heart sank. An emergency or a wounded crew. Was it

*Over Exposure*?

The battle-damaged B-24 skidded to a halt, emergency crews immediately responding, and Reed could tell from a distance it was not the plane with which he was most concerned. Where was Lieutenant Forshay? The planes landed, one by one, and finally he spotted *Over Exposure* rolling to a stop, apparently safe and sound. Shaking his head, he stalked over to the debriefing building to see what the hell had happened.

# Chapter Ten

As the first child of three siblings, Patricia Prentiss was the darling of her family and the apple of her father's eye. Born in the quaint town of Bath in 1918, she grew up in an idyllic setting, the town peppered with Roman artifacts, bridges and baths, wide green expanses for cricket matches, gentle undulating hillsides, and quaint shops. She loved listening to the locomotive's whistles as trains came and went along the nearby railway, imagining the places they'd go.

Growing up, she reveled in the built-in history the town offered, and immersed herself in studies, discovering a penchant for language early on. The Russian revolution fascinated her as she advanced through school, and she was widely recognized as a future scholar by many a teacher and her headmaster.

Her father, Guy Prentiss, had served and survived the Third Battle of Krithia at Gallipoli in early June of 1915, suffering several wounds including the loss of three fingers on his right hand that left him constant reminders of Churchill's folly. No fan of the stubborn man, he'd hoped England had seen the last of him. Little did he imagine that his precious, intelligent daughter would one day be caught up in another of Churchill's plots.

Patricia grew up in an almost embarrassingly charming row house a few blocks from the River Avon, and not too far from the Oldfield School where she prepped for her continuing education at St. Hugh's. Popular and outgoing, things just seemed to come to her easily, without much need to study. Given that, she was less than fully prepared for success at St. Hugh's, a place where upon her arrival she dealt with a bit of culture shock mixed with no small amount of homesickness and lack of proper study skills.

Powering through those difficulties with traditional British fortitude, the young Miss Prentiss did indeed assimilate over time, learned how to hit the books properly, and went on to learn multiple languages. She rapidly became admired for her inborn ability to quickly discern priorities and solve problems, and had an uncanny knack for knowing what to say under pressure. In fact, the last quality saved her and a few of her chums from trouble with the local authorities more than once.

After a year at St. Hugh's, she had demonstrated a knack for enjoying life at the limits of decorum along with a pint of beer now and then and brief, non-committed dalliances with students of the male population.

Far from the typical dowdy intellectual, Patricia reveled in the freedom her intelligence gave her – freedom to think and do almost anything she pleased, uncomplicated by many of the archaic rules and norms expected of proper, quiet British schoolgirls. Among her milder indiscretions, she and two of her contemporaries infiltrated an anniversary dinner at The Queen's College, an ancient six-hundred-year-old school of Oxford, by joining the last row of the choir in singing the school's traditional Latin grace:

*Benedic nobis, Domine Deus, et his donis, quae ex liberalitate Tua sumpturi sumus; per Jesum Christum Dominum nostrum. Amen.*

The girls sang loudly and off-key from the first note, while the horrified traditionalists in the audience didn't dare to look up from the prayer to see who had sullied their time-honored, sacred event. As the "amen" hung in the air, the three girls escaped, laughing uncontrollably, scampering through a nearby side exit, directly into the custody of a stern-looking bobby, poised by the exit steps.

Insisting they had been invited by the choirmaster, supposedly the uncle of one of the girls, but not having had time to properly prepare or rehearse, Patricia stated with conviction that the girls ran from their embarrassment rather than face the scrutiny of the ill-tempered audience. Thumbing one's nose at centuries of tradition, especially at such a revered institution was not highly thought of, and could easily result in a stern lecture if not outright expulsion from school. With a wink though, they were let go with an admonition to confine their frivolous activities to the halls of St. Hugh's.

By the time the school was requisitioned for the British military in 1940 as a treatment center for wounded soldiers, Patricia was on her way to a career in hospital administration, and so the use of the school for healing head wounds was not unwelcome to her, as she stayed on to assist with the transition, organization, and operations.

Patricia rose to the task with determination and compassion. There was no lack of variety of wounds. A man with his cheek and eye socket shot away. Another with no lower jaw and another with his nose and upper mouth mangled. There were more, plenty more. Brave men were maimed for life and many were grateful to still be alive. Others failed to embrace such optimism and would have preferred to die instead of carry on through the recovery and disfigurement. It was a matter of how one viewed the glass of water. The horrific wounds suffered at the hands of Hitler's troops filled Patricia with a resolve to do whatever she could to help defeat the Nazi menace. She was capable and more than ready to serve in any capacity.

In the quiet, dark hours when men were alone with their thoughts, she'd visit and softly chat, whispering visions of hope and beauty, whatever came to mind. For the ones who were able, she'd offer the additional comfort of a tender touch. Depending on their response, she would go further, just like she had with the boys at Oxford, delicately offering a relieving massage if they responded. She felt quite sure of the therapeutic value, carried absolutely no guilt about it, and took no small pleasure from the act herself, thinking back on the multiple visits she'd made, later in her room.

It was at St. Hugh's that a mid-level official with the SIS doing extended debriefing sessions with a few soldiers and airmen reunited with the brilliant administrator, the clever, beautiful one who was fluent in the Russian language and had an advanced ability to think on her feet.

A former patient at St. Hugh's himself; Joseph Sterling had been a handsome, virile flying officer and an excellent Spitfire pilot. Credited with fourteen kills of the ME-109 German fighter and several JU-88 bombers, Sterling also flew the Hawker Hurricane, a less nimble plane but a more stable gun platform for attacking the bombers. The Battle of Britain raged on for some four months as the Royal Air Force desperately fought off the Luftwaffe. Sterling made it though unscathed until mid-October when his number finally came up taking cannon fire from a swooping 109 that caught him from behind and below. He crashed his Supermarine Spitfire in a cow field somewhere west of Chelmsford after helping stave off yet another Nazi air attack. The crash left him badly wounded with a sharp tear from the left side of his mouth back to his ear, along with several broken ribs and a lacerated spleen.

After a month of initial treatment, Joseph Sterling was dispatched to St. Hugh's for further treatment and recovery, making the acquaintance of the very comely Miss Prentiss. Unlike other staff at St. Hugh's who looked away at the sight of him, Patricia Prentiss looked in his eyes instead; looked into his soul. For that he was both humbled and grateful. They chatted about Brighton, where Joseph grew up and Patty's adventures and mildly scandalous behavior at St. Hugh's before the war.

The impression she left on him lasted for several years, as he moved on to a position with the SIS helping with cryptology development. Unsuited for further flight duty, his knack for numbers got him in with the very secret and vitally important MI6. It was there that he came to the attention of a certain Colonel Melkin who had a habit of retaining virtually everything he heard or saw. Colonel Melkin canvassed his contacts including the promising Joseph Sterling to see if anyone had knowledge of a qualified female who spoke Russian and might be a worthy candidate for a special operation.

# Chapter Eleven

Lieutenant Fred Forshay had gained the attention of Colonel John Reed on advice from "Sir" Colin Nichol of the *King's Head* pub in the early fall and was recommended by the SIS agent for Colonel Melkin's mission. Shortly thereafter, Reed arranged for Lieutenant Forshay to meet Miss Prentiss and by design, the two hit it off quite well, according to Reed's plan.

When on a subsequent mission the young pilot skillfully brought back a shot-up B-24 and executed an emergency landing on two engines, a partially collapsed nose wheel, and barely operable hydraulics, Colonel Reed knew in his gut Forshay was the right man for the job. The mission was flown in one of the "borrowed" ships they used when *Over Exposure* needed extended repairs. Maddy had fired a flare from the co-pilot's window as they came in view of the field at Wendling, indicating an emergency. Truly, it was. The lives of the entire crew were in Freddie's hands. He did not disappoint them.

During debriefing, Colonel Reed was impressed with Fred's cool demeanor and the casual way he described the mission.

"Tell me about your bomb run from the IP," Reed asked as he leaned forward across the well-worn wood table.

"Well, it sure wasn't a milk run," replied Fred, curling his lip in a confident smirk. "Flak was heavy and accurate, and we took quite a few holes and got bounced around a lot, but no one was injured."

"What were the conditions over the target?"

"Cloud cover was four-tenth's I would say. Feinstein had a clear view so we dropped on the primary with the rest of squadron." Fred took a deep breath and looked past the Colonel's head to no particular point on the wall.

"We saw Lieutenant Miller's ship take a direct hit on the right wing, "Freddie paused and looked down at his shoes. "They didn't have a chance."

"And then what happened?" Reed asked as he shifted in his chair. He was an intelligence guy, not a flyer. The bravery, the valor of the crews... He wanted a taste of it.

"Well, we made our turn and that's when we took a hit on the number three engine. It conked out right away. After that, we got out range of the flak and we were jumped by 109's."

"How many were there?"

"It's hard to say. They were all over us for a few minutes before the P-47's got into the mix. We took a lot of bullet holes on the left wing and lost number one."

"So you made it all the way back on just two engines?" Reed was almost flush with excitement, imagining himself on the flight deck, struggling to keep that big bird in the air.

"Yeah, uh yes sir, it was kind of rough but we managed to reach the channel. I thought we might have to bail out but she kept going long enough to make it back to base. So we did."

"I debated whether to have the crew bail out before I landed but there really wasn't any time and I didn't think I could make altitude, so we all rode it in. The landing was pretty rough but the ship held together, and here I am talking with you." Fred was growing impatient.

"Well, we're all glad you made it back in one piece. I think your plane is salvage, though. Get something to eat and get some rest. I think you've earned a day or two off."

"Thank you, sir. Let me know if you

think of anything else." Fred stood up smartly and left without remembering to salute. But Reed didn't notice or mind. Not only was he going to put Lieutenant Forshay up for an Air Medal, he was able to confirm he'd found his man for the SIS mission. He called Miss Prentiss right away to let her know of his final decision.

Fred walked briskly to the Nissen hut. He wasn't hungry, he was shaking. The stress of the mission finally caught up to him. Let the others go for chow. He needed a few minutes alone, where no one could see him sobbing uncontrollably, all the while squeezing his lucky shrapnel piece in his hand as he eventually fell asleep. A short while later, there was a knock on the door. Who in the world could that be?

"Enter!" Fred shouted his response and quickly wiped his face.

"I have a note for you, sir." The sergeant, a youngster unknown to Fred didn't even look up at him, so Fred didn't have to come up with some excuse for his red eyes.

"Thank you, sergeant." Without being dismissed, the sergeant turned on his heel and hustled away to do some other menial task. He didn't like being a messenger boy or matchmaker. The nice lady had said it was important, and asked that he hand-deliver the note, so he did.

"Get cleaned up, and come see me at the *King's Head*," the note said. It was from Patty. More of a demand than a request, really. While he hadn't known her long, he already knew she could be that way. Fred's heart raced a bit, and his mood began to elevate. Although they had only spent time alone together once before, it was more than Fred could have imagined, and he looked forward to seeing her again.

Fred got cleaned up, put on fresh clothes and grabbed his lucky shrapnel piece before heading over to the duty hut to check out and grab a bicycle. The *King's Head* was a ten minute ride away, plenty of time to think of something clever to say, and time enough to imagine Patty's full lips on his own, and maybe elsewhere, later. It made him twitch.

The pub was busy, flush with locals and airmen looking to forget the horrors of flying in battle and perhaps to find a friendly companion, though the odds were never good for the latter.

The *King's Head* pub was an ancient place, and the building was one of the oldest in the area. It squatted on a corner of the main road through the village, offering sanctuary and a pint or two for tired farmers and anxious American flyers. The pub was shaped as if someone had laid a rectangle on top of half an octagon, creating a gently curving wall facing the street, and a larger, square room in the back towards the bar.

Outside, a wrought iron frame held a slightly crooked, colorful but faded sign with a caricature of King Henry V supposedly, the monarch well regarded for his stunning victory at the Battle of Agincourt in 1415.

The village of Wendling was not much more than a hamlet, really, situated among a patchwork of farms, in a wide open space in County Norfolk, with expanses of rolling land quite suitable for a military airfield. In fact, the whole of County Norfolk and almost every suitable strip of land in the region known as East of England was dotted with 8th Air Force bases and airfields. It was the logical launching pad for the thousands of B-24's, B-17's, and a variety of escort fighters as they pounded Germany and German-held interests into submission.

The field itself was just north of the

village, close enough so that anyone living there knew when a mission was being launched or planes were returning. Many locals said a quiet prayer every time they heard the engines fire.

The *King's Head* served as a meeting place for the small village council, a welcoming sanctuary for farmers who wanted a quick pint and sandwich at midday, and also for many of the pilots from the nearby airfield who wanted some kind of normalcy and to get a fleeting sense of home. A bit further from base than similar facilities in Beeston, it was not quite as busy and therefore something of a refuge from the terrors of the air.

Fred parked his bike near the others and walked in, remembering to doff his cap lest he risk the rancor of the assembled crowd and possibly having to buy the house a round. He spotted Patty sitting on a low bench near one of the windows on the outer octagon.

Patty looked radiant in a smart dark blue dress that revealed a little of her ample chest. She reached up to him for a kiss as he approached, holding the kiss a second or two longer than necessary.

"So, how was your day?" Fred smirked a bit, taking her a bit by surprise with his offhand remark.

"Aren't you the chipper one for having crashed a plane this afternoon?"

"Nothin' to it." Fred borrowed his ball turret gunner's favorite phrase.

"Do they get mad at you when you break one of their planes?" Patty smiled teasingly as she put a cigarette to her lips while Fred reached for a match.

"Oh, the Germans broke it," Fred replied. "I just brought it back for repairs."

They both chuckled a bit even as Fred recalled the terror of the exploding flak all around him. He reached for his lucky shrapnel piece in his pants pocket for reassurance.

Fred excused himself to the bar to retrieve a couple of pints, nodding at Colonel Reed who had stationed himself in a dark corner near the end of the half-circle bar. Curious, he thought, that the Colonel should be here, too.

"Here's to another successful attack on Herr Hitler," stated Fred in a voice that drew a few cheers from the other patrons. Halfway standing in salute, he and Patty touched glasses in a toast and drank lustily from their heavy mugs.

Fred's pronouncement jump-started a raucous drinking song, one that was gloriously put into motion by an inebriated navigator from the 578th. Everyone soon joined in.

> *When de fuehrer says*
> *We is de master race*
> *We pfft pfft pfft*
> *Right in the fuehrer's face*
> *Not to love de fuehrer*
> *Is a great disgrace*
> *So we pfft pfft pfft*
> *Right in the fuehrer's face*
> *When der fuehrer says*
> *I gotta have more shells*
> *We pfft pfft pfft*
> *For him we make more shells*
> *If one little shell*
> *Should blow him straight to hell*
> *We pfft pfft pfft*
> *And wouldn't that be swell*

After the boisterous song ended and the cheering died down, the pub returned to its normal clatter. Patty looked into Fred's bright and eager eyes.

"Now, mister, is there anything I can do to ease your stress from such a harrowing day?" She emphasized the word "harrowing" while coyly smiling at her favorite pilot.

Fred looked up over the top of his glass, stopping in mid-gulp. She didn't mince words. No one did really, in such desperate and precious times.

"I've got an itch you could scratch." Fred was as good as Patty when it came to playing cat and mouse. Only he wasn't sure if he was the cat or the mouse. In the end, it didn't matter, if what he hoped was going to happen, actually happened.

Colonel Reed watched them but could not hear the conversation from his station at the bar. He saw that they were getting along quite well and not wanting to be any more obvious, paid his tab, nodded to Sir Colin Nichol, who winked back at him, and headed for the door. Sizing up the young couple by the window, Colin drew two more pints and brought them to the table.

"Courtesy of the Colonel."

Fred drew an uneasy sigh, not at all sure what to make of today. Finishing the first pint, he began the second, trying to stay in the moment. The "moment" was across from him at the small table. Her light brown hair cradled her oval face like a gold frame shows off a precious painting. Love or lust, he wasn't sure, but for the moment, he was content.

Back at the base, Sergeant Gene Jordan had Spencer out for a long walk in the dwindling daylight. In a little while, he'd find out from his buddy in ops if the repairs on *Over Exposure* were complete. Never one to trust such an important chore to someone else, he wanted to clean and check the ball turret guns himself. No sense in risking fate to a faceless mechanic.

Letting the memory of today's frightful mission fade, Gene was content to park himself near the stump of a tree and enjoy the fact he was still alive and breathing. His hand idly rubbed behind Spencer's ears as his thoughts drifted to home and family.

Spencer's nose was working overtime and as he barked at a shadow in the nearby brush, several quail leaped into the air. Gene thought back to the days not so long ago, when he would hunt ducks with his uncle Jeremy. He instinctively tracked the quail's brief flight, wishing he'd had a twelve-gauge. Of course at this distance, the shot would turn quail into hamburger. It didn't matter. He was weary of the war and not much of anything mattered. He'd had enough of it and wanted to go home. In the pages of a calendar it hadn't been that long, just four months, but God, it seemed like a full lifetime had passed.

He thought back to all the missions they'd survived, including the time they'd gotten separated from their squadron, found a group of B-17's and helped them bomb some target near Ludwigshafen. When things didn't go according to plan, you made a new plan.

Gene closed his eyes and leaned back against the tree. They were getting closer to making the quota of thirty-five missions. It seemed well within reach, and at the same time it seemed like there was no chance in hell they'd survive until then.

Colonel John Reed strolled back along Beeston Road to the air base. The little matchmaking effort between the newly minted British spy and his own hand-selected pilot seemed to be paying off, and he contemplated this as well as the other mission details along the way. It wasn't a terribly long walk, less than a couple of miles, and it gave him time to go through the plan once more in detail.

Although his counterpart, British Colonel Reg Melkin had conceived it, many of the details were up to Reed – the pilot, the crew, and the specific timing. Things had to move along rapidly though, as Operation Frantic was not exactly making any headlines with the brass and was in danger of quickly folding. Churchill wanted access to the Russian airmen and this was his best opportunity.

The main worry that haunted Colonel Reed was being found out before he could execute the plan. Melkin had appealed to his sense of history by trumping up the potential significance of the mission, and urged him to work as a single agent within the 392nd Bomb Group to make it happen. Not even the base commander could know. It wasn't at all a proper observance of chain-of-command but such trivialities were not a concern of the SIS or other spy services.

If the mission failed, Forshay, his crew, and the girl would simply be victims of war. If it succeeded, it would be Reed's ticket to a bright future in counter-intelligence operations. He was sure of it, and now he was sure of the proposed target he could use to inject his plan – the upcoming triple back to back to back daylight bombing missions to Cologne. It was to be an all-out assault on the industrial complex located on the upper Rhine. It would be exceedingly busy at the base, a great time to pull off the mission. Time was running short, too. He was under pressure from Melkin to get the mission off before Operation Frantic totally fell apart.

At the last possible moment, he'd reveal the final details to both Lieutenant Forshay and Patricia Prentiss, and only then would Fred know they'd been secretly paired for the mission. For the time being, they were free to grow fonder of each other, as Reed wanted.

*Over Exposure* would be fitted with a device Melkin's folks had developed to spray combustible oil droplets on the hot engine manifolds, creating huge plumes of smoke. It would work long enough for the plane to simulate battle damage and turn away from the bomb run. The devices would be placed in two of the engine cowlings in the early morning hours while the crew's were being briefed. They would be triggered by a long wire running to the pilot's seat where Fred would fire them off at the appointed time.

Pretending to turn for home apart from the main group, *Over Exposure* would descend out of sight, and then turn east for Ukraine and Poltava airfield. The only thing the American commander at Poltava would know is that a B-24 was coming in with a special VIP visitor, an expert in infirmary operations, to offer assistance not only to the American contingent but to the Soviets as well, as a goodwill measure. Lord knows they needed some goodwill between the supposed allies.

After Miss Prentiss was introduced to the Soviet general, a formality which would be de rigueur for such an important guest, she'd no doubt be invited to his offices, where she'd find a way to get the proof Churchill wanted. The B-24 would be refueled and readied for the shuttle return, and off they'd go. If everything went to plan, of course.

To explain the missing ship, Fred would land it at Brussels emergency landing strip number fifty-six on the way back, as if they had landed there directly from the Cologne mission. With the help of the local ground agents and the Belgian underground, everyone would be hustled back to England on a transport plane and *Over Exposure* would be salvaged on the spot by local operatives of the SIS.

Fred's crew would be held back from the first run at Cologne but they'd fly the second day. That way, the ground crews would be too busy working on the planes that returned from day one to notice any unusual activity on *Over Exposure,* and it would have already been prepped for the second day's flight.

It was not a perfect plan – there was no such thing in war – but it had a good chance of working.

As to his spy getting the information, while the "what" was clear, the "how" wasn't. Colonel's Melkin and Reed were counting on Patricia Prentiss' natural ability to think and perform under pressure and to improvise. The 392nd and Lieutenant Forshay would get her there. Melkin's people would provide her with a vial of chloral hydrate to drug the general – "slip him a Mickey" as they would say – but if the opportunity to apply it didn't present itself, she would need to create one or come up with an alternative on her own.

She'd think of some way to find out just how much the Russians knew about secret American flying technology including the deadly accurate Norden bombsight. Churchill had to know what he was facing as he thought ahead in preparation for World War III.

# Chapter Twelve

Finishing his second pint of beer, Freddie rambled on about a dog he had growing up, how his father refused to pay for any food and made the dog sleep outside, even in the rain and cold. She let him go on, knowing that it was a good way for him to unload a different unpleasant memory and thus help soothe the nearly unbearable emotional wounds of combat. She reached over and gently touched his hand.

"Freddie darling, are you quite done with your beer because I feel the need for a good long backrub." She said this while circling her index finger around the top of her own empty glass. Freddie knew from their first encounter that a backrub was a euphemism for something else that involved her back – her backside, that is. He was up for the idea in seconds.

Snapping out of his reverie, Fred felt two sudden urges. One was for a quick visit to the loo to get rid of the beer he'd just borrowed. The other was to find relief from the other urge, using the exact same vessel.

"If you'll wait here for a moment, I'll be right back to escort you to your flat and make arrangements for that uh, backrub."

Sighing heavily, Patricia looked out the window. It was getting dark now, and in just a while, she'd have her American lover ride her roughly from behind, like it was for the last time ever. It very well might be. A shadow appeared on the table. She looked up.

"This package is for you," said Sir Colin the proprietor. He nodded, knowingly. "Special delivery from Colonel Melkin." In the envelope was a small aluminum cylinder with a secure, screw-on top. Instinctively, she knew it was the chloral hydrate solution. She calmly slipped the small vial into her purse.

The time must be drawing near, thought the British spy. A British spy... who would have thought that back at the Oldfield School? What would her father think? He'd disapprove but secretly he'd be proud and at the same time greatly worried about her safety. Waiting for Freddie to return, Patricia's mind wandered back six weeks or so, recalling how she'd gotten herself into this mess.

After plucking her from St. Hugh's and prior to shipping her off to work with the infirmary at Wendling, the SIS had provided Patricia Prentiss with a two-week, rudimentary basic training class consisting of some hand-to-hand defensive tactics, as much background on General Kaminsky as they could muster, and a very broad overview of the mission including what documents to look for after she wormed her way into the Russian's private office. A worthy student, she assimilated everything like a sponge soaking up a spilt glass of milk.

She was already quite adept at thinking on her feet and the SIS counted on that and her other innate skills to get the job done. They didn't provide a great amount of detail about the general's aggressive sexual proclivities but did advise her to not be surprised if he made an advance on her – after all, it was the source of his weakness, the one the British sought to exploit. Decorum prevented going into greater detail and so it was sort of a "nudge and wink" moment. Both men assumed their young spy would catch their drift.

As Melkin and the others knew already, Miss Prentiss was more than capable of handling herself and put their full trust in that knowledge. What they didn't know is that if this general seemed worthy of her, she might make the first move herself. Just to take him off guard, of course. The thought of taking the role of a seductive spy gave her a warm sensation that made her yearn for Fred's touch even more.

The details of the exact timing and the mission participants had been omitted but after the first "chance" meeting with Lieutenant Forshay, she started putting two and two together. She'd be paired up with the handsome and brave American pilot and his crew, and then shuttled off to meet the general, get the intelligence Churchill wanted, and become the hero Melkin and Reed wanted. As Freddie would say, "Nothin' to it."

She also saw through Colonel Reed's rather thinly disguised effort to incite a romance with Freddie and she didn't mind. Fred was a nice young man if somewhat gullible, and he knew how to make her feel good. There were precious few opportunities to feel good thanks to Hitler, and she intended to make the most of each one, vowing at the same time to do her part to put an end to this madness, if she could.

Grabbing her hair and pulling her head up and back, Fred finished with much more urgency than their first time together. No doubt, the danger he'd flown into earlier in the day manifested itself in his release. Patricia moaned with him, enjoying the mild roughhousing just as much as she had enjoyed teasing her young pilot. Miss Prentiss was a real handful and she met him move for move, unlike the few other women he had known.

Freddie moved to get up from Patty and she corrected him almost sternly, commanding him to stay exactly where he was. She rhythmically squeezed him with her insides for several minutes, extending their mutual pleasure, including several waves that coursed through her from her ankles to her shoulders; pleasurable aftershocks to the fleshy earthquake.

After a few moments that seemed to Fred like a heavenly weightlessness, the lovers pulled apart from each other. Flopping over on the bed, Freddie breathed heavily, hoping to God to survive the upcoming mission so he could spend another evening with his new friend. At least one more evening.

At the same time, Patty hoped Fred would go out of his way – well out of his way – to make sure she was safely transported home, no matter what. Men at war fought for a few things – for freedom, for country, and for the loving embrace of a woman who knew what she was doing in bed. Patricia Prentiss was definitely, supremely, one of the latter.

# Chapter Thirteen

Henry Thomas and Dolores arrived at the antique mall at the same time most days, to prepare the store for the daily activities including turning on all the lights, setting the sidewalk display items in place, opening up the register, logging in to the computer system, and of course, putting up the quaintly lettered "open" sign.

The mall was actually converted from an empty grocery store spanning ten thousand square feet and host to about thirty different dealers who paid Henry Thomas a fee to display and sell their wares. The mall had hundreds of thousands of items, from primitive hand-hewn wood scoops to vintage or mid-century modern furniture. A visitor could find old cameras, reclaimed industrial parts, antique jewelry, dolls, and plenty more.

Wednesdays were usually slow, but this day, a gentleman was waiting as they unlocked the door at 10:00 am. It was the older man who had been in a week earlier looking at the World War II flight log. Before unlocking the door, Henry Thomas turned to Dolores at the front desk.

"I told you he'd be back. Do I know my customers or what?"

Dolores just shrugged. He did have a

knack for predicting what people would ask for, would buy, and which ones would wander the store for hours only to leave empty-handed.

"Good morning," Henry Thomas said brightly. "Please come in."

"How are you today?" Gene Jordan was dressed in a white golf shirt, yellow sweater vest and khaki slacks. Very Palm Beach.

"Are you back to take another look at the flight log you saw last week?" Henry Thomas was curious.

"Well, yes I am, and I'd like to apologize for just storming out the other day. That was impolite of me."

"Not at all," replied Henry Thomas. "I just hope you're OK."

"Yes, I'm fine. It was just a shock seeing that book. I'm pretty sure it belonged to my pilot back in World War II. I was a ball turret gunner on a B-24. My name is Gene Jordan by the way."

"Really!" Henry Thomas' interest was at full maximum now. "I'm Henry Thomas and this young lady is Dolores. So tell me about the book."

"Well, how about if I buy you a cup of coffee," he nodded to the Dunkin Donuts across the parking lot.

"That would be fine. Dolores, I'll be back shortly." He took the log book from the case and brought it with him.

They walked over to the donut store and stood in line. There was always a line. Gene ordered a black coffee and cruller and Henry Thomas limited himself to coffee, two sugars. Picking up their order, Gene motioned to the couch by the window. This might take longer than Henry Thomas had planned. He glanced back towards the store. Dolores could handle things for a while.

Henry Thomas took the log book from its silk case and handed it to Gene. "Tell me about it," gesturing to the small book.

"Well, let me see." Gene opened the small notebook as if it were a fine family bible. There were thirty-five entries, comprising the first thirty-five pages of the book. The rest were all blank. There was nothing to classify the book as having belonged to someone in particular, and no record of the unit, squadron, or bomb group. It was not embossed with a squadron logo nor did it have any scrap of identifying information.

"Yes, I'm quite sure this belonged to Captain Forshay." After all these years, Gene still referred to the lieutenant as "captain."

"The missions match up. It's all here. No two crews ever had the same exact missions." His eyes grew a bit damp as he studied the writing. The ink was still as dark as it was when first applied to the paper. Gene rubbed a finger under his eye – he didn't want to cause a run in the ink with a stray tear after so many decades. He exhaled slowly and sat back on the couch.

"This book hides a big secret, "sighed Gene as he looked Henry Thomas in the eyes. "In fact, it hides a couple of secrets."

"Go on," Henry Thomas replied, sipping his coffee and trying not to seem overly anxious. Truth is, he lived for historical intrigue and this sounded like it could be good.

"We had a few milk runs, but we sure had some rough missions, too." Gene stopped at a particular page. He was not ready to tell Henry Thomas any secrets, not just yet. "Here, look at this one."

The writing was crisp; the description was succinct and elegantly brief. Pilot log entries have always been short and to the point.

*Mission #20: September 12, 1944, to Hanover, longitude 9°48', latitude 52° 25' N. Bombed oil refinery. Heavy, accurate flak. Hydraulic system shot out. Nose tire shot up. Crash landed at base. No one injured.*

Henry Thomas let out a low whistle. "That must have been rough."

"It was one of the worst. Captain thought we might have to ditch in the English Channel or maybe parachute out over the base but he couldn't get enough altitude so we rode it in."

"And you were so young," Henry

Thomas observed.

"Well, we grew up pretty goddamn fast, I can tell you that," snorted Gene. "Captain flew us back on two engines and landed that bird on brute strength, him and the co-pilot. We all walked away."

Gene Jordan's lip quivered just a bit as he sighed heavily. "Freddie saved every one of us that day." He took a bite from his cruller and washed it down with coffee, trying to stifle his shaking hand.

The pair was silent for a moment as Gene relived the Hanover mission yet again and Henry Thomas tried to imagine having lived through that one experience, much less thirty-five such missions.

"You said something about a secret?" Henry Thomas couldn't contain his curiosity any longer.

Gene pursed his lip, hesitated, and then relented. "Flip through the book until you get to October 15." Gene sat up taller on the soft couch. "Got it?"

"Here it is," murmured Henry Thomas. "Mission to Cologne."

*Mission #30: October 15, 1944 to Cologne, longitude 7° 0' E, latitude 49° 37' N. Bombed marshalling yards. Heavy accurate flak and rockets. We had #1 and #4 engines knocked out, #2 and #4 gas tanks and cross feeds knocked out. 2 cylinders on engine #2 knocked out. Had quite a time. Couldn't use radio or shoot flares. Crash landed in Brussels, plane a total wreck. No one injured.*

Henry Thomas sat back on the couch and let the air out of his lungs. He looked at Gene and back at the page. "It's hard to imagine anyone survived something like that." He shook his head softly as he read the entry one more time.

"Well, the only part of that log entry that's true is the target assignment and that we landed in Brussels."

Henry Thomas turned his head slightly and looked over top of his reading glasses. His face asked the question as he leaned forward.

"Let me tell you about something called 'Operation Frantic.'"

# Chapter Fourteen

Winston Spencer Churchill hated Bolsheviks. Hated them. Bolsheviks, Communists, whatever you wanted to call them, he referred to them as a baby that deserved to be strangled in its crib. It started with Lenin in 1917 when the Germans let him (gave him a ride even) return from exile to lead the fledging revolution, hoping it would distract the Russians from the war effort. Within seven years, Lenin was dead, replaced by the head Bolshevik, Josef Stalin, who had cultivated his relationship with Lenin and his position to assume outright and complete leadership of the Soviet Union.

Churchill and the Americans were fully cognizant of the fact the Soviet Union was going to be a major force in world politics after the war. What power would they possess? How would they use it? Just as Churchill was worried about Stalin, Stalin was worried about the Americans. He was jealous of their superior technology and worried about how and when they would use their power.

The uncomfortable alliance between Britain, the Soviet Union, and the United

States was actually a war within the war. The feigned cooperation was center stage several times as the "big three" met at the Cairo Conference and again at the Tehran Conference. It would show up again later at the upcoming Yalta meeting and then at Potsdam. Churchill trusted Stalin about as far as Franklin Roosevelt could carry him on his back.

Sipping his customary glass of water with a splash of Johnnie Walker Red, accompanied of course by a seemingly ever-present cigar, Churchill contemplated the folly called Operation Frantic.

The Americans wanted it badly, but Churchill saw no value in it. The notion of "shuttle-bombing" German targets had some merit, but having to trust the Russians as part of it was unacceptable. He wanted nothing of it. The U.S. also sought to develop a base in Siberia, to launch attacks on Japan. Logistically, it was absurd but so was America's very presence in the war. The endless convoys and flights, the ferrying of materials and personnel. Such resources, so much resolve. The vast capability of the Americans was hugely impressive and the implications it carried were neither unrecognized by Josef Stalin nor underappreciated by Mr. Churchill.

Surrounded by wisps of cigar smoke, Churchill thought more deeply about the operation, sitting back in his leather chair in the Annex at 10 Downing Street. He sighed, made a few notes, and summoned his current secretary, Miss Astley. Joan Astley was Churchill's trusted administrative officer really, a much larger role than simply a secretary, called upon to accompany the British leader to the major summits with Roosevelt and Stalin.

"Get me Menzies, will you?"

Stewart Menzies was the head of the SIS, also known as MI6, the super secret group focused on myriad wartime efforts but with a long history of finding out everything they could about communism and the Soviet Union. Churchill wanted to know all about the Soviet commander for Operation Frantic and he needed a Russian-speaking spy for a special operation he had in mind.

# Chapter Fifteen

Operation Frantic was aptly named, for a variety of reasons. It could have properly described the arduous task of getting Stalin to agree with the concept, an effort that lasted half the war. It could have been used to describe the nightmarish logistics required to build three air bases in remote central Ukraine, shuttling every nut, bolt, gallon of gas, and tent across the ocean to Murmansk, then by train through Eastern Europe, or by the Air Transport Command through Tehran. It could have referred to the somewhat disjointed missions, meant to prove the concept worthy of the massive effort.

From steel mesh runway sections to the last soup pot in the base kitchen, the airfield at Poltava was constructed on land generously offered by the Soviets, a spot recaptured from the retreating Germans. Along with this largesse, they also insisted on providing base security, a serious flaw in the American commander's plan, but one that Stalin's general insisted upon. Similar facilities were built at two other locations situated along the battered Soviet railway at Mirgorod, and Pyriatyn.

Stalin finally agreed to the operation in early February 1944, and by June, the first mission was launched. The hasty completion of three bases plus the deployment of thirteen-hundred personnel was a masterful logistics feat by any measure. That the Americans could actually pull it off so seamlessly caused Stalin no small amount of concern. In fact, it alarmed him like nothing else had done previously. The rapid deployment capability of the westerners could cause immense damage to his Eastern European acquisition strategy.

On June 2nd, one hundred thirty B-17's and seventy P-51 Mustang fighters of the 15th Air Force left Italy, and bombed marshalling yards in Hungary with the bombers landing at Poltava and Mirgorod, and the fighters at Pyriatyn. Four days later they mounted an attack on an airfield in Romania and returned to Ukraine, and then on the 11th, the shuttle run was completed with a bombing run at another Romanian airfield, returning all planes to Italy. The first shuttle-bombing mission was complete, and by all estimates proved the concept. The staff at Poltava celebrated, the brass back home were impressed. The euphoria however was to be short-lived.

Gene Jordan got up from the comfy couch to fetch another round of coffee as the story about Operation Frantic played out. Henry Thomas called Dolores on his cell phone to let her know they'd be awhile. It was a typical Wednesday with just a customer or two so far, so his absence would not be a problem. Besides, it gave the nosy store owner something to do while Dolores busied herself with brain-teasing games on her new tablet.

Gene settled back down on the couch and continued to explain Operation Frantic. Mind you, he knew virtually nothing about it as it was happening, but years after the war, he'd studied it quite a bit, and felt proud about his own limited and unique participation.

# Chapter Sixteen

With one hugely successful shuttle-bombing mission in hand, mission planners were eager to launch the second attack under Operation Frantic. Sustaining the effects of shuttle-bombing operations was crucial to gaining sufficient time to learn more about Soviet logistics, their technological capabilities, and their ability to conduct air bombing campaigns. In fact, the value of Operation Frantic was not so much in the shuttle-bombing missions – after all, many targets were already within reach of bases in Italy – but for gaining intelligence about the Soviet's capabilities to fight the next war. At least that was the plan. Over time though, it became clear that their Communist allies trailed far behind the US in technology, process and tactics so little was gained other than affirming their shortcomings.

Soviet commanders were eager to learn as much as they could about American technology too, with a number of senior officials at work pumping the Americans for anything of value that they could steal and use for the advancement of their own forces. Such was the cat and mouse game between the two world powers as the defeat of Germany became more obvious.

Studying the precepts of Operation Frantic, Stewart Menzies recognized the opportunity Churchill was seeking. As head of the SIS, he had the access and the tools to go and get what Churchill wanted. His man to execute the plan was none other than Colonel Reg Melkin, his former roommate at Eton, a decorated combat leader and well-regarded spy if there was one and one who had deep access to a number of useful American contacts.

Melkin's plan was simple and elegant – identify a female operative who could gain access to General Kaminsky's private office and determine just how much intelligence the Soviet's had gained at the American's expense. He needed someone articulate and fluent in Russian, capable of thinking on her feet, and charming at the same time. Where better to look that the scholastic hallways of Oxford?

With success by the squadrons based in Italy, the second shuttle-bombing mission would now test the ability to carry out operations from England. It was the 8th Air Force's turn to bomb going out and coming back. The June 21st mission consisted of one hundred forty-five B-17's and no less than one hundred forty fighter escorts, including P-51's, P-47 Thunderbolts, and P-38 Lightning aircraft. The massive formation's objective was to bomb a synthetic oil plant at Ruhland, and then proceed to the three airfields in Ukraine for refueling, reloading, and a second bomb run on the way back to base. It would be an otherwise ordinary mission with the exception that the force would continue eastward to the new bases in Ukraine instead of turning around and heading back to England. The force's failure to turn for home and instead continue on eastward was not lost on the Germans.

After bombing the synthetic fuel plant and nearby marshalling yards as a secondary target, and surviving some fierce air-to-air combat involving a couple dozen Luftwaffe fighters, the massive force headed for the three Ukrainian bases, with just one B-17 lost to combat. The Germans suffered six airplanes lost with one P-51 being downed during the skirmishes. While the P-47's and P-38's returned home, a force of sixty-four P-51's escorted the bombers to Ukraine, landing at Pyriatyn with its shorter runways while half of the B-17's landed at Poltava and the other half at Mirgorod. Operation Frantic was enjoying its second success, but any celebration was to be quite short-lived.

The Luftwaffe had become aware of the American bases in Ukraine but lacked specific information. Nonetheless, a force of JU-88 twin-engine bombers, plus Heinkel He-111 medium bombers was assembled at German bases in and around occupied Minsk, hoping for an opportunity to strike the new American bases.

The opportunity came in the form of a lone He-111, trailing the formation of B-17's unnoticed, following the force directly to Poltava in Ukraine. With the location of the base now in hand, the Germans wasted no time in launching an attack.

Before midnight, the German force was spotted crossing into Soviet territory heading towards Poltava, and while it gave adequate time for the bomber crews to take shelter in the trenches surrounding the airfield, the advance notice did nothing to help the woefully inadequate Soviet defenses. Limited to truck-mounted .50 caliber machine guns that the Soviet commander had insisted would be sufficient to defend the base, the anti-aircraft fire was wildly ineffective during the ensuing raid, with no German bombers lost in the attack.

As midnight came and went, German long range He-177 Pathfinder planes located the exact position of the Poltava airfield, stuffed to the gills with more than seventy B-17's, waiting to be plucked like flowers in May. Some were parked in protective revetments but others were more vulnerable, out in the open. The pathfinder planes came in first and flares were dropped directly over the target, making the bombing runs by the JU-88's and He-111's deadly accurate. The bombardment lasted for nearly two hours, and nearly all of the B-17's were destroyed or severely damaged.

The American casualties were light with

two pilots lost during the raid from injuries but the Russians lost plenty, as commanders ordered firefighting crews to the field while bombs were still falling, to put out fires on the precious B-17's and to disable hundreds of "Butterfly" anti-personnel bombs. The bravery of the Soviet men and the lack of concern for their safety by their commanding officers were both impressed upon the visiting Americans.

A day that had seen great success over the target area in Ruhland ended in disaster with something as simple as a single German plane following the bomber force to the base at Poltava. The ring of Russian .50 caliber guns helped map out the base perimeter for the German pilots, who relentlessly destroyed the force of B-17's, making the disaster at Poltava one of the worst losses of American aircraft during the entire war.

With only two missions in the books, Operation Frantic had turned from unbridled success to unmitigated disaster. The only silver lining in the dark cloud surrounding Poltava belonged to the Russians. It was the fact that among the ruined B-17's lay a wealth of surviving American technology, including the highly guarded Norden bombsights. By ordering his men to fight fires while bombs continued to fall, General Kaminsky had secured the ability to recover several of the prized targeting devices. Amid the resulting turmoil and cleanup, there was no chance whatsoever the Americans could know that some of their secret equipment was missing or in this case, stolen.

A third Hero of the Soviet Union medal was surely awaiting the officer who seized such advanced technology. General Kaminsky's chance meeting back in 1935 with the young German airman Willy Antrup, the Oberstleutnant who nine years later led the Poltava attack, was proving to be quite fruitful. In times of war, doing what one had to do regardless of the uniform or manifesto could be quite useful for one's career development. So a few dozen of his men lost their lives in the effort. Each of their families would receive a letter attesting to their extreme bravery in the face of the horrendous surprise attack by the hated Germans. He would personally see to it.

"Wait, you're telling me that this General..."

"Kaminsky."

"This General Kaminsky tipped off the Germans so they could bomb his own airfield?" Henry Thomas was incredulous.

"I'm just saying what some of the research showed me," replied Gene Jordan. "Some people think that he did tell this Antrup guy all about the Americans, just so he could get his hands on some of the Norden bombsights in the confusion of a bombing attack. How else would the

Germans have known to shadow that particular bombing force to Ukraine? "

"Well, I wouldn't put it past the Russians, especially in that time period, but to call in a bombing attack on your allies and kill dozens of your own men?" The sentence hung in the air unanswered like an early morning fog.

"So, where you in on that mission?" Henry Thomas was now leaning forward, the fingertips of one hand touching the other forming a "V" shape with his hands. He was clearly enthralled in this historical mystery.

"No, heck that was before I even got in theater," replied the old ball turret gunner. "We came along a month after that."

"So what happened next?" Henry Thomas was hooked on the story about an operation he'd never even heard of in spite of his extensive reading about World War II.

"Well, from what I could tell, the whole operation kind of went into limbo right after that. Only two missions into it and it was already starting to fall apart. Far as I could tell, there was not much intelligence to gather about the Russians, either. We had them licked in technology, protocol, strategy, you name it."

"But Churchill still wanted information about the Russians."

"Right, and so by the time they came to us for the secret mission, there wasn't much left of it, just a half-crew at Poltava, and not much for them to do. By that time, things had gotten pretty ugly between us and the Russians."

After the disaster at Poltava, fewer than a dozen B-17's were fit to fly from the base. The rest were destroyed outright or beyond repair. It was a calamity. The morning after the attack by the Luftwaffe, Operation Frantic leaders directed the surviving B-17's at Poltava and the ones at Mirgorod and the fighters at Pyriatyn to immediately depart for bases further east. It was the right move, as the Luftwaffe attacked the two remaining bases later that day, finding empty runways and causing little damage.

The harm had been done, and victories were claimed by the Luftwaffe as well as by General Kaminsky, the proud owner of four Norden bombsights to go with the other intelligence he had gathered from his visitors over glasses of vodka. As fires burned at his airfield and time-delay Butterfly bombs continued to maim his troops long after the attack was over, he carefully packed up three of the prizes along with the associated autopilot equipment for a trip to Moscow. He kept the last one in his office as a trophy. It would look good mounted in a case in his parent's home in Vyshelej. After the war, of course.

Within a week after the Poltava raid, the remaining B-17's and fighters from the earlier

June raid assembled in one group and bombed marshalling yards and an oil refinery at Drohobycz Poland on the way to a temporary stop in Italy. Waiting for weather to clear for a return to England, the B-17's joined in with the 15th Air Force on an attack on marshalling yards in Romania while P-51's joined up to attack a variety of German targets in Hungary. Finally, as the weather cleared over England, the group returned home, bombing marshalling yards in France along the way. Technically, they were shuttle-bombing as designed but with half the original force lost, the second Operation Frantic mission could only be described as a total failure.

"So, was that end of it?" Henry Thomas was trying to connect the dots between the early attacks and Gene Jordan's mission, of which he still knew nothing about.

"No, there were a few more missions over the summer, but nothing special," replied Gene. "Fighters flew the next two missions in July and August of that year. Minor actions, really, just to keep the concept alive."

"No more bombers?" Henry Thomas was totally confused.

"Oh, there was another bomber mission on an aircraft factory and then the Russians asked the US to bomb an oil refinery in Poland, which we did."

"So the operation continued."

"Sort of. By August there was a big uprising in Warsaw with the Polish Home Army. They were having some success against the Germans and wanted our help but the Russians wouldn't let us use the bases in Ukraine."

The Polish Home Army was one of the largest resistance movements in Europe during the war, with up to six hundred thousand members at its peak. The Warsaw uprising in the late summer of 1944 was in danger of collapsing under the weight of superior German materials and men. The Poles begged for help, and Churchill pleaded with the Americans and Soviets to give aid.

Stalin would have none of it. He wanted the ability to control Poland after the war and a strong Poland would make it all the more difficult for him. He also did not want the Americans establishing any more of a foothold in Ukraine than they already had. He refused permission when asked to allow relief missions from Operation Frantic bases. Finally, after relenting to one mission, the US flew a high-level airdrop of relief supplies with clearance granted to fly over Soviet airspace. After the supply drop however, they were not allowed to land on Soviet territory. American commanders were furious.

Eventually, the resistance was crushed with thousands of Polish fighters killed and ten times more civilians murdered by the Germans in mass executions. Only after the Soviets overran Poland near the end of the war, did Warsaw and elsewhere receive relief from the German invaders. One ruthless occupier had been replaced by another though and the bitterness towards the Russians felt in Warsaw, a city almost totally destroyed, was matched by ill feelings at 10 Downing Street and in the Oval Office in Washington. One more straw could break the camel's back on Soviet relations.

Operation Frantic continued into early fall with two more missions, bombing oil refineries on the way out and arms factories on the way back on the sixth mission, and on the seventh mission, B-17's dropped over twelve hundred containers of supplies for the Polish Home Army, flying in from England, and landing at Poltava in spite of the objections from the Soviets. Only two hundred fifty or so of the containers actually reached the Polish forces.

"Did I tell you that the Russians shot at our planes?" Gene looked over at Henry Thomas who was trying to absorb all the information about Operation Frantic.

"Wait, what? What do you mean they shot at our planes?"

"Turns out they were pretty notorious for shooting at anything that flew nearby," continued Gene Jordan. "They were kind of trigger happy and if you didn't stay right within the approved airspace and the time allowed, you were getting shot at. Sometimes, they'd shoot at our guys even if they were on time and where they were supposed to be."

At Poltava, the start of fall was also the start of increased trouble between the Russians and their American guests. The facility was a mess. The infrastructure was archaic and the Russians seemed to have little incentive to do things the right way. It was both curious and infuriating to the Americans. There was not a lot of intermingling, partly due to the configuration of the base with the Americans posted at one end near a cluster of revetments and the Soviets at barracks well down the runway to the east. The Russians also occupied several administration buildings and a regional infirmary treating wounded soldiers. There were random physical attacks by Russians on the Americans, usually when they could get the drop on a lone soldier or as part of a joint event where insults and eventually fists and weapons were used. Something had to give.

Rumors were everywhere about rapes and even murders on the Russian side of the base. The American officers developed a deep mistrust of their Soviet hosts and it became the bad seed to future relations. Behind it all and doing Stalin's will was General Kaminsky, urging his junior officers to let the men run wild, even rewarding them for some of the mischief caused. After all, he had what he wanted and no longer needed to play polite host to the westerners. They were no longer and indeed never were welcome in the first place. It was becoming mayhem, and without any active air missions to support, both sides grew itchy for a fight.

"I had no idea." Henry Thomas was perplexed.

"Neither did I," replied Gene. "Not until I saw firsthand what was going on there." He'd thought like most Americans that the Russians were close allies during the war. At least that's the pabulum that was force-fed to the unsuspecting public by the United States government all during the war when in fact, the complete opposite was true.

# Chapter Seventeen

Winston Churchill was glum. One couldn't tell by his facial expression, a nearly perpetual scowl with worry lines and creases that were first formed more than two decades ago with the disaster at Gallipoli and the fighting in the trenches of France. The blitz in 1940 had forced him out of his regular residence at 10 Downing to the more secure annex though it was hardly bomb-proof itself.

No, years of war had taken a toll on Churchill's face and his demeanor but he powered through it all with unfettered determination. He'd make sure to smile for the press when he was intentionally seen in public. It helped bolster the morale of his countrymen. But one worry seemed to be replaced by another, and as 1944 began its final few months, he was not so much worried about the Third Reich as he was the Red Menace. The Allies were slowly taking back Western Europe but the Russians were pushing hard from the east. It was their ultimate intentions that had the prime minister worried.

Operation Frantic had nearly disintegrated and he still hadn't been able to get the SIS operative in place to verify his fears of the Russians having gained access to sensitive US technology. In fact, the Russians and the

110

Americans were at each other's throats. The window of opportunity was nearly gone on Colonel Melkin's plan. Something had to give.

Truth be told, SIS was stretched beyond any reasonable limit, dealing with multiple problems, including the Russians. Although Churchill had a variety of intelligence to support his fears, he wanted proof that the Reds had gotten hold of American bombsights and maybe other technology. While their air force was not currently a challenge, he knew that a post-war Soviet Union could quickly ramp up production of highly effective bombers, especially with secrets stolen from the allies. If the blitz had been bad, Winston Churchill shuddered to think what armadas of Russian long-range bombers could do. He rang up Menzies.

"Stewart, what can you tell me about your Poltava operation? Can we get it done?"

"Mr. Churchill, we have selected a target date and it's coming up quickly. We have the people in place."

"Well, what's happening there? I hear the Americans and Russians are fighting with each other on a daily basis."

"Sir, the flight operations have basically died off, so there's not much for them to do. The Americans have started to pull out their personnel, but we still have time to insert our agent."

"Well, let's get it done. I have to know."

"Yes sir, we believe we have the right cover story and the right person to pull it off."

"Going in as something of a peace maker, are you?"

"Yes, mister prime minister. Our agent has actual experience in hospital administration and we're going to offer our assistance to both the Americans and the Russians to help them establish post-combat treatment centers and we're going to offer to set up an example at Poltava. A goodwill gesture if you will. An olive branch of sorts."

"Well, do what you can Menzies. I'm putting my faith in you."

"Thank you, sir. We have every reason to believe this will succeed."

Skipping any formalities, Churchill simply hung up the phone and reached for his cigar. Menzies would get it done. He was sure of it.

# Chapter Eighteen

Lieutenant Fred Forshay was in the briefing hut precisely at 0530 on October 14, the date of the first of three missions to Cologne. It was obviously going to be a full effort with thirty-six air crews being briefed and planes from the 576th, 577th, 578th, and 579th all scheduled to go.

"Men, your primary target will be the marshalling yards at Koln. Remember, the Cologne Cathedral is right next door, and we haven't damaged it yet, so let's keep that record intact." The briefing officer went on with some details that would be of more interest to the navigators as Fred's mind drifted to his last encounter with Patty. She was a British tiger and he was her willing accomplice.

"Any questions?"

Fred was jolted back to reality.

"Lieutenant Forshay, please stay behind to meet with Colonel Reed. Everyone else is dismissed."

With that, the assembled crew members stood to attention as the brass departed, then quickly followed them, heading to the flight line and the revetments scattered around the five-sided airfield that held their aircraft. With the planes scattered about the base, there was little chance of any one enemy attack destroying a majority of the bombers. According to the chatter of the crews, this was going to be one bitch of a mission. Cologne was heavily defended.

As the crew of *Over Exposure* arrived at their plane, they were met by the head of the maintenance group, called the Sub Depot, a captain who had been serving at Wendling since January.

"This plane is not flying today, gentlemen." He sounded serious.

"What are you talking about?" Gus Fletcher knew the plane was in fine shape and ready to go. "There's nothing wrong with this ship."

"All I know is that the plane is not ready to fly, and you are all to stand down." Having delivered his message as directed by Colonel Reed, the Sub Depot captain departed for other urgent matters.

Confused and slightly embarrassed to be leaving the mission to their fellow airmen, the crew of *Over Exposure* headed back to their barracks. Gene Jordan fetched Spencer and took him for a walk. One less mission today meant one more on some other day. It didn't bother him either way. Gus grabbed his trusty Argus C3 and went off to capture some photos taking advantage of the long shadows and the early morning light. A few of the others simply went back to bed.

Maddy, navigator George Feinstein and bombardier Robert Roberts went to find Fred to see what the hell was going on.

Fred's face was slightly ashen. This was it. All he knew up to now was that he was to fly a special mission past German occupied land to Ukraine to deliver a VIP passenger to an American air base. He was about to find out a lot more.

"Lieutenant, can you find your co-pilot?" Colonel Reed needed to brief both of them, along with the navigator, Lieutenant Feinstein. After all, the safety of the crew and the success of the mission itself relied on some pinpoint flying through the restricted Soviet airspace.

"Yes sir, I'm pretty sure they're all looking for me, wondering what's going on. So am I, frankly."

"We'll get to it shortly. Please find your co-pilot and navigator."

Fred didn't have to look far. The three other officers were waiting outside the briefing hut.

"Mother and George, we need you inside. Colonel Reed wants to speak with us."

"What about me?" Roberts the bombardier protested his exclusion.

"Just wait for us here, OK?" Fred tried to hide his annoyance.

Robert Roberts, the man with two first names, scuffed his shoes in the dirt and turned away.

"Gentlemen, thank you for being prompt and I apologize for the sudden scrubbing of your mission, but I have another mission for you. Something of the utmost importance."

The other men knew of Colonel Reed and had spoken with him at times during some particularly intense debriefings but knew little about the man. Fred knew only a little more. The two men looked at Fred, wondering what he had been keeping from them.

"Lieutenant Forshay knows about the mission but none of the details yet. That was for a reason. Now, I'm going to tell you all at once, and as you know, nothing of this conversation leaves the room." He stared into each of their eyes, looking for any signs of weakness for the task. Satisfied, he continued.

Reed looked up and signaled for Colonel Melkin who quietly entered the room and swiftly closed the door behind him.

"Gentlemen, this is Colonel Melkin of the British SIS, their intelligence arm. Colonel Melkin."

"Yes gentlemen, Colonel Reed speaks very highly of Lieutenant Forshay here and his crew. I am counting on you to pull off a rather ambitious mission. To Ukraine."

Ukraine! What was in Ukraine? Maddy and George looked at each other, then at Fred, then at the British Colonel.

"As Lieutenant Forshay is aware, your ship will be ferrying an important VIP guest to an American base at Poltava in Ukraine. The base and two others have been part of an operation that conducts shuttle bombing missions, flying out from England or Italy, bombing their targets, and then landing in Ukraine."

Feinstein had heard something about the operation but kept his mouth shut. He learned though, that getting in and out of those bases was no cakewalk.

"The planes are refueled and reloaded and then they bomb another target on the way back to base. Kind of a two for one deal if you will. Am I clear so far?"

The three officers nodded in unison.

"Very well. This operation with the Soviet military is coming to a conclusion but we have a special need to insert our guest to do some much needed goodwill with the Russians. Relations have shall we say, become quite strained and our goal is to try and help patch things up."

No one believed that was the real reason for a high risk mission, but no one dared speak.

"Uh sir, who will be flying with us?" Maddy was wondering about fighter escort.

"Actually, you'll be on your own into and

out of Ukraine."

The mission was starting to sound pretty sketchy to the young crew.

"Well, how are we going to do that, sir?" Feinstein felt a twinge of apprehension. Every other mission he'd flown had been with dozens of other planes around him plus the always welcome escort fighters. This sounded like needlessly risky business.

"In fact, you'll be flying out tomorrow with the rest of the 392nd on the second mission to Cologne."

There would be a second mission to Cologne right after this one! Nothing like tempting fate with German 88mm flak guns.

"The difference is you'll leave the group as you reach the IP after feigning battle damage and retreat from view before heading east to the Poltava airfield."

"Could you explain further, sir?" Fred was now beyond curious.

"You're going to be flying Tail-end Charlie in the last group. You'll fake two engine fires, fall back from the group, and circle around to the north before turning towards Ukraine." The other crews will assume you've gone down over the target.

The men looked at each other. The room was silent. Colonel Melkin studied their reactions before he spoke.

"Look, I know it sounds a bit cheeky but we have reason to do it this way. That's about all I can tell you."

"Who is our VIP passenger?" Fred wanted to know exactly who was so important that they had to go through all the cloak and dagger to get him into Poltava. It had better be worth it.

"Colonel..." Melkin turned to Colonel Reed who nodded towards the adjutant standing in the hallway near the window.

Turning towards the opening door, Colonel Reed spoke. "Gentlemen, let me introduce you to Miss Patricia Prentiss, our special guest VIP for this mission. She'll be working with our team at the Poltava infirmary and will be a special liaison to the Russian counterparts. Relations are falling apart there and we need to remedy that quickly, for several reasons. Miss Prentiss is well qualified to mend some fences on both sides of the base by offering some newly developed treatment methods for the Russian wounded."

Freddie's jaw dropped. Maddy and the navigator looked at each other, mouths open, eyes darting from Fred to the lovely guest, and back to the Colonel.

"Miss Prentiss, I believe you've already met Lieutenant Forshay." The colonel couldn't have been more disingenuous.

"Yes, "she replied. We're familiar with

each other." Emphasizing the word "familiar" only heightened Fred's confusion. What the hell?

"As Colonel Reed was saying," Colonel Melkin continued, "Miss Prentiss is something of an expert in hospital administration and is fluent in Russian. We hope that she will help restore some friendly relations with the Soviets and help them establish better treatment facilities for their wounded soldiers so we can get on with winning this war together. It is a diplomatic visit really, with no small amount or urgency I might add. If she succeeds, then we'll have set the stage for more positive relations with the Soviets as the war draws to a close. If not, then the fewer that know about it the better." It sounded plausible.

"Sir, why can't Miss Prentiss simply take a transport flight from Iran?" Fred inherently knew there was more to the mission than Melkin was letting on.

"Well, that's a bit of a problem, Lieutenant Forshay," the colonel replied. "As I said, we can't have half the Army Air Corps talking about this, can we?"

Fred wasn't buying it, especially the notion that a British hospital administrator could help patch things up with the Russians when their complaint was with the Americans but he had no choice. In spite of that strategic flaw in the plan he and his crew were already in deep and so he said nothing further.

"Right. After Miss Prentiss completes her meetings, you will ferry her back home, with the exception of a detour in Brussels."

"The emergency landing strip," commented Feinstein.

"Exactly. We'll need to explain why your plane disappeared from the bombing run, so you'll land at emergency landing strip fifty-six and be ferried back to Wendling by a transport flight." It was not terribly uncommon for a disabled bomber to land at one of the emergency landing strips that dotted the landscape. As the Allies advanced, temporary landing strips were built along the way. Rather more permanent and more secure facilities were constructed to handle cargo delivery and wounded personnel transport.

"What about *Over Exposure*?" Maddy demanded to know.

"Your ship will be salvaged for parts at the emergency field and you'll be assigned a new ship upon your return."

More silence. "Of course, this mission and everything I've said today will remain a secret from this moment on, do you understand?" Heads nodded.

"Do you *understand*?" The colonel was red in the face.

"Yes sir, we understand." Fred, Maddy and George all agreed, as did Patty.

"That's all you need to know for now.

Lieutenant Feinstein, my aide will give you the details for navigation so please stay behind. You will fly out tomorrow. Any questions?"

All four of them knew better and all shook their heads no.

"Say nothing of this meeting or this mission. Am I clear?" Colonel Reed got in his two cents. More nodding of heads.

"Lieutenant Forshay, I will give you details on what you need to do and what you can tell your crew this afternoon." Colonel Reed brought the intensity level down a bit with his easy drawl.

"Thank you, sir." Maddy and Fred stood and saluted, looked briefly at Patty and left. Fred's eye caught Patty's for a long moment, and then he looked away. Patty sighed. It was going to be a hell of a trip.

# Chapter Nineteen

"Buy a girl breakfast?" Patty caught up to Fred and Maddy. Maddy looked at Fred, then at Patty and said something about the infirmary and left in a hurry.

Fred looked incredulous. "How can you be so nonchalant about this?"

"Sounds like a what do you call it? Oh, a milk run."

"You're out of your mind." Fred walked faster. He was annoyed, felt betrayed even and didn't want to talk, especially with Patty.

"Where are you going?" Patty tried to keep up.

"Anywhere away from you," came Fred's sudden reply.

"Now, wait!" Patricia Prentiss was riled up. "Why are you mad at me?" Fred stopped in his tracks.

"You don't think this whole thing – us - was set up by Melkin and Reed?"

"Of course it was. I saw it a couple of weeks ago. I couldn't say anything to you, you know that."

"Look, I don't like being used, that's all." Fred was boiling over, nearly in a rage.

"Fred darling, you're being used every day you go on a mission. How is this so different?"

Fred shrugged and put his hands in his pockets. He looked down, then back up at Patty, gathering his thoughts. Then he spoke slowly and calmly.

"Colonel Reed set me up to care about you, right? So I would make sure you got through this little mission in one piece. Does that about sum it up?"

"Well I suppose, but if he hadn't chosen you, he would have made a similar arrangement with some other pilot. Is that what you want?"

Fred turned his head and pursed his lip, only not in the confident way he did when flying with Maddy, but in a resigned way. He was completely frustrated.

"Look Patty, I don't know what's going on right now. I need to be alone." Fred paused for a second. "OK?" It wasn't a question. It was a demand.

Without waiting for an answer he marched off to his Nissen hut, leaving Patty standing in the morning shadows, unsure of her next move. She thought he'd be excited about going on this great adventure together but unlike her, he didn't appreciate the sheer and dramatic magnificence of it all.

Well, after all the drama, Fred would calm down and realize the mission came first. He was too good a pilot to feel otherwise. His reaction though gave her pause. It was rather a slap in the face really. She started walking off the base. Now what?

The answer came a little while later in the form of a short but virile looking young American enlisted man walking her way with a very British looking dog on a tight leash. He seemed not to have a care in the world. Patty hesitated a moment but decided that an idle diversion was just the thing she needed at the moment to soothe her hurt feelings.

"Your dog is adorable." Patty bent down to greet Spencer and rub behind his ears, a move the dog greedily accepted, snorting his approval.

"Uh-huh." Gene Jordan was slightly bemused by the interruption but didn't let on.

"Does he have a name?"

"Spencer. Like Winston Spencer Churchill."

"Oh, lovely. He kind of favors the prime minster a bit, don't you think?"

"Well, I know he's a good dog and I'm glad to have him," replied Gene, curious now, and playing the interaction close to the vest.

"Could I walk him for a bit?"

With no other particular destination in mind and no chores to do, Gene wanted to see where it would lead. He handed Patty the leash and Spencer responded with a strong tug.

Patty smiled that endearing, come-on

smile she'd perfected while attending boy-girl parties at St. Hugh's. She'd entertained a number of young men in the past by starting the mile race at the half-mile mark. It still worked, she thought. Lieutenant Forshay and his worries and oversensitive reaction would have to take a back seat to her new interest.

"He's pretty strong for his size. So are you, I imagine."

There it was. The come on. She was a fast worker, thought Gene. He'd seen it before. War time made for cutting through all the bullshit quickly and getting right to the point.

"Let's just say I can handle myself," Gene responded with youthful honesty, a big smile and unabashed self-confidence.

They walked a bit, letting Spencer lead them off the base property and towards town. Gene had nothing to do with the mission having been cancelled. He didn't even care why other than it meant the crew of *Over Exposure* had lost a day towards meeting their final goal. Some other day they'd fly another mission. For now, it was a pleasant morning stroll and an easy conversation as they exchanged the basics – a first name, a bit of background about Gene's shooting abilities, some banter about the upcoming winter months.

"I have nothing to do the rest of the morning, how about you?" Patricia went straight for the jugular.

"I'm off today so I'm as free as a bird." Gene was not as naïve as his age might let on. He'd been with one girl before enlisting and war had a knack for knocking any remaining innocence out of a person pretty quickly.

"Maybe you could indulge a needy young woman with a backrub."

"Wait." Henry Thomas interrupted Gene as he told of the brief encounter. "You mean to tell me that you slept with the woman your pilot was seeing?"

"She came on to me. I didn't know she was involved with our captain or what she was up to. Not at the time, anyways. It didn't come up. I don't think she knew I was a member of his crew either. I thought she worked at the base or something and was just lonely. It was worth it, though. She was a real handful."

The mid-morning light slanted through the sheer curtains, enough to light the room fairly well. Spencer slept fitfully on a corner of the rug in Patty's small flat while his owner sat on the bed, pants around his feet as his new friend eagerly but slowly pulled on him. Knowing full well that the young American flyer wouldn't last more than a minute or so, she quickly brought him to his first release. It was the second one she was more concerned with, when he would last longer and provide her the return satisfaction she sought. Seeing his pleasure filled her like a dam waiting to burst. Gene didn't disappoint, responding to her gentle touch a mere ten minutes after he'd taken his first flight.

Patty whispered in his ear and told him exactly what she wanted the eager airman to do. Obediently he followed her instructions, like a recruit marching to the cadence of a seasoned and demanding drill instructor. Do this, don't do that so fast. Grab my hips. Patricia was right. Gene took much longer the second time and filled her needs as she insisted. Later that day, standing toe to toe, their matching height made the goodbye embrace and deep kiss even more comfortable and sweet. He'd remember this morning forever. He hoped for a repeat visit. If he survived of course.

# Chapter Twenty

Reg Melkin and John Reed sat in a small private room at the *King's Head*, a single-malt whisky in front of the British Colonel and ale of no particular distinction in Colonel Reed's hand. The pub was officially closed for the afternoon but they were having a special meeting, waiting for "Sir" Colin Nichol to join them after he finished his bar duties.

The old Colonel opened the door and both men stood respectfully, in deference to the highly decorated First World War hero. He was sought out by the SIS years earlier to be a local source, a "finder" if you think of it, of information, people, activities... anything that could be of value to the war effort, especially so close to an American air base. He'd gladly obliged and eagerly accepted the monthly stipend to supplement his admittedly modest bar earnings.

"It's a go," declared Melkin, looking at Colin Nichol and then at John Reed who nodded in affirmation.

"So this Forshay fellow is going to work out for you?" Colin wanted feedback on his selectee. After all, he'd picked the confident young pilot out from the scores of others, first tipping Reed to his views and then together, they suggested the pilot to Melkin for his special mission.

"Yes, he'll do quite well," replied the British agent. "He's survived this far and he's a remarkable pilot from what I've been told."

"And he's taken a shine to our young Miss Prentiss," added Colonel Reed, stating what all present already knew. Nichol thought it unnecessary and Melkin was ambivalent. Whatever Reed thought it would take to ensure success was alright with him.

"Right. So they're off to smell out the Russians tomorrow and in a few days, we'll have the answer Mr. Churchill wants." Nichol sounded hopefully confident even though he wasn't exactly sure what it was Miss Prentiss was pursuing. Not every detail had been shared.

"Well, we'll have an answer," replied Reed, "But we're not sure what it's going to be."

They all nodded solemnly and fell quiet for a moment as Melkin and Reed drank. As they paused, Colin stroked his red goatee and looked out the window at a young airman walking a dog. There was a young lady walking with him. They stopped and spoke a few words, then went their separate ways.

"Isn't that Miss Prentiss?"

Both of the active duty Colonels whipped their heads around to spot the couple as they parted ways, and then looked at each other with no small amount of alarm.

"I knew she had an eye for men," mused Colonel Melkin, "But isn't that man a member of Forshay's crew?"

"Yes, he sure is," replied the American colonel. "I wouldn't worry too much. They'll be airborne in fifteen hours. Nothing can happen between now and then." He made a mental note to have someone posted to watch her flat overnight. No sense in tempting fate. Fate was doing quite a good job on its own already.

Colin Nichol stepped out for a moment and returned with a small glass of gin, raising it to his guests. "Cheers!"

"Sweethearts and wives," added Colonel Melkin, studying his glass. They all drank to king and country and to Fred Forshay and Patricia Prentiss and *Over Exposure*.

Walking slowly back to base with Spencer sniffing a variety of things along the way, Gene Jordan whistled softly thinking of his remarkable encounter. His stomach growled at him, reminding him that he'd missed lunch in favor of something else that was quite satisfying. In fact, he'd performed three times that day, the last one a lazy, drawn out coupling he and "Patty" enjoyed, relaxing with him spooning her from behind, as they both took pleasure from her unique and quite wonderful squeezing motions. He'd never felt anything like it, and frankly at his tender age, there were plenty of things he hadn't experienced. He was looking forward to another afternoon with her, and hopefully a long and productive life back home after this damned war.

"Spencer old buddy, I hope you liked that woman. I think you're going to be seeing more of her before long." Might as well be optimistic.

Henry Thomas sipped the last of his coffee and leaned forward on the couch. The lunch regulars had already come and gone from the "double-d" and Gene was hinting that he had to leave by checking his watch three times in the last five minutes. Besides, Mary his Uber driver was waiting outside in a cream-colored Nissan Rogue.

"Will you come back and tell me the rest of the story?" Henry Thomas was hooked. He had to know what happened next.

"Well, you hang on to that flight log and hunk of shrapnel for me, OK?" Gene was adamant. "Don't go selling it to anyone else."

"Of course," replied the shop keeper. "I'll lock them up as soon as I get back to the store."

"When are you coming back?"

"Maybe next week. I have some doctor appointments." With that vague answer Gene got in Mary's car and they left. Henry looked at the book in his hand and hefted the oddly shaped piece of shrapnel in his other. What other stories did these two artifacts hold? He couldn't wait to find out.

# Chapter Twenty-One

Ten days had passed since Gene Jordan last visited the antique shop. Henry Thomas was itching to know the rest of the fascinating story and had read through the flight log several times marveling at some of the other mission descriptions Lieutenant Forshay had penned.

*Mission #8: August 6, 1944 Hamburg, longitude 10° 0' E, latitude 53° 35' N. Bombed an oil refinery and storage tanks. Heaviest flak barrage I've seen. Also rockets. Got quite a few flak holes.*

*Mission #13: August 16, 1944 Kothen, longitude 12° 0' E, latitude 51° 50' N. Bombed JU88 engine factory. Heavy accurate flak and rockets. Quite a few flak holes. Saw B-24's and B-17's going down like flies.*

Henry Thomas shuddered at the thought. Never in the military, he nonetheless held service men and women in the highest regard, World War II veteran, Korea, Vietnam era, or Middle East. They were all revered in his eyes.

It was a busy Saturday at the store with a steady flow of customers unlike the slower weekdays. The phone rang. It was Gene Jordan.

"I thought you were coming back for a visit," hoped Henry Thomas. "I've been looking forward to hearing more about your mission."

"Can't make it," replied Gene in a raspy

voice. My doctor has me on house arrest for a while. Some test result he didn't like, so I'm stuck here for now."

Henry Thomas thought for a moment and almost didn't ask the question he had in mind.

"How about if I come visit you?" Silence.

"I'll bring the flight log and shrapnel and some deli for lunch."

"OK, that's fine," replied Gene. "Get a pencil and I'll give you directions. But save the lunch, they'll feed us here."

Taking notes, Henry Thomas told Gene he'd be up on Monday, typically the slowest day at the antique mall. He hung up, and looked up to see a short line of customers patiently waiting to check out. It was not the type of store where people were in a rush. Henry Thomas turned to his task all the while thinking of Gene and the next revelation from his mission to Ukraine.

The portico at Gene's assisted living condominium was attended by a middle-aged Haitian gentleman, an employee of the facility for the past twelve years, well accustomed to helping folks in their golden age with the patience of Job and a deaf ear to some of their unkind remarks. It was a good job and some of the residents remembered him generously at the holidays. It was enough to be helping people. He knew full well that his time was not that far behind theirs.

Henry Thomas nodded to the smiling

doorman as he was directed to the reception desk. Gene had told him to meet him in the card room. Why they had a card room with so many tables never made sense with so few players. It was a quiet place and they'd be left alone.

Gene Jordan sat upright, dressed as usual in muted pastels, and impeccably groomed. Henry noticed there was a cane leaning on his chair. That was new.

Henry Thomas reached out a hand and the two exchanged greetings and small talk about the warm weather for a few minutes.

"What do you think of the place?"

"It looks quite comfortable. The doorman is very friendly." Henry Thomas was being polite. He dreaded the idea of ever having to move to some place where strangers assisted you in daily living.

"Well, it's not so bad," Gene replied his voice not as cocksure as it was at other times. "Don't forget, there are about three women here for every man," he added with a wink.

Henry Thomas just smiled. Of course; the lightly staffed facility could not possibly keep track of every resident all the time. The old guy was getting some after all these years. What had Patricia Prentiss unleashed decades ago?

Henry Thomas was a little impatient. "So, we left off with you having had an uh, encounter with the Prentiss woman. Before your mission to

Ukraine."

"Yes, that's right. You know, whenever I can't perform, I think back to that day and bam!"

Henry Thomas shifted in his chair, a bit jealous that this old man seemed so profoundly able to do what he himself had difficulties with from time to time. Perhaps he was just exaggerating a bit.

"So yeah, the mission was the very next day. I was still smiling when we headed out to the flight line."

Overnight, Melkin's men had attended to the smoke devices on engines number one and four, as planned. It was slightly more awkward to rig two triggering wires to the pilot's position, so they rigged one to the pilot and one to the co-pilot. The preparations went off smoothly and no one noticed anything unusual. The Sub Depot's crews were hastily completing repairs on no fewer than twenty B-24's from the day's mission to Cologne. In only a few hours, the very same target would be attacked and the ships had to be airworthy. They would be ready – it was a matter of pride to the ground crew. A serious matter, and so a couple of mechanics scampering about a B-24 in the moonlight meant nothing to anyone but the watchful eye of Colonel Reed. Just the same, he'd vaguely enlisted the confidence of the Sub Depot captain, telling him he was installing some kind of special camera for intelligence purposes in case there was an inquiry. Their work complete, the two men simply nodded to Reed as they walked past his jeep.

It was an early day with crew briefings at 0330 and 0445. Fred Forshay listened without interest, focusing on his own briefing; the one Colonel Reed delivered personally last evening. Fred had slept fitfully; still pretty sure he was not being told all the gory details. If he were Colonel Reed he wouldn't have revealed every detail either. Get the woman to Poltava, let her do what she needed to do, keep the crew safe and ready to go, get the plane refueled and checked out. Be ready to leave on a moment's notice and then land in Brussels as planned. How hard could it be? Still, something was unsettling. It had to be more than a simple diplomatic mission as the Colonels had said. It must be something pretty damned important to fake the shooting down of an American B-24 bomber. Something was not right about it, not right at all.

Maddy had taken the second briefing at face value. Why complicate things more than they needed? Besides, he knew about Fred and Patricia and was just stunned that she was being shuttled off to the barren Ukraine for some diplomatic purpose. Maddy was not one to question orders; he preferred to follow them. Someone had to help keep an eye on Fred. He was flying his bedmate into an unknown situation including the ever-present dangers of simply flying in formation and risking flak bursts. George had his navigation instructions; he and Fred knew the basic plan. They'd do their job and chalk up another mission. Drop bombs or ferry a VIP... it was one more mission off the list.

The crew of *Over Exposure* was driven out to the usual revetment on the south corner of the five-sided airfield. Again they were greeted by an officer. A Colonel.

"Men, your mission today as you know, is Cologne. There will be a slight change of plans however. Lieutenant Forshay will explain." He wanted to make sure the pilot didn't reveal too little or too much, and it was his confirmation that Forshay had a grasp on the plan.

"Alright, this is a secret mission we're going to be on, so no one says anything to anybody, not today, not in thirty years. Got it?"

Heads nodded nervously.

"We're going to fly 'Tail-end Charlie' in the low formation today." Tail-end Charlie was the lowest and furthest back plane in the combat box; a location that would make their subterfuge less noticeable. There were groans from the crew. Tail-end Charlie was perhaps the most vulnerable spot in the otherwise reasonably well-protected box formation of bombers. The density of the bombers, although not as closely spaced as the easier to fly B-17's was designed to provide effective cross-fire from multiple guns against any marauding German fighters. It was easier to get picked off in the last and lowest position.

"When we get to the IP, we're going to be dropping out of formation and heading to a US airfield further east, in Ukraine."

Men leaned forward, each with a surprised look, waiting to hear more.

"We have a VIP passenger already on board. We are to deliver her (HER?) to this base and wait for her to complete a sensitive diplomatic mission, and then we'll return home. Any questions?"

The men looked at each other quizzically. No one spoke. Gene Jordan just shrugged. After all, he was just fifteen hours or so removed from an unexpected encounter with a lovely British girl who had seduced him, and rather brashly.

Colonel Reed nodded his approval. Whether or not Lieutenant Forshay really believed that this was solely a friendly diplomatic mission was beside the point. So long as that's what he convincingly conveyed to his crew, the mission was properly positioned for his purposes.

"Good luck, men. We'll see you back here in a couple of days. Lieutenant..." Reed accepted a salute and hopped into the waiting jeep. Forshay turned to his crew and looked into their eyes. They were on board with the plan.

"Well, let's go."

"So, you didn't know that it was Miss Prentiss on board your plane?" Henry Thomas was trying to keep up with the story.

"Nope. Not a clue. Imagine my surprise when I saw her sitting on a flak jacket next to the radioman's station."

The men clambered aboard *Over Exposure*, eager to get on with the mission. The sooner they got started, the sooner they'd get back, and maybe they'd dodge the heavy flak barrage expected over Cologne in favor of the diplomatic mission. It didn't make a lot of sense, but a lot of things made little sense in war, so this was their mission and as always, they'd do their best. Simple logic, simply applied.

Gene Jordan entered through the open bomb bay and headed forward across the narrow catwalk to sit with the radioman Sergeant Withers, his normal routine for takeoff before getting into the ball turret after the squadron formed up. Some ball turret gunners preferred to sit with the waist gunners and frankly, all the turret gunners had a spot for takeoff and landing other than their turrets. He squeezed between the bombs and what he saw shocked him to the core.

Sitting cross-legged on top of a flak vest sat Patricia Prentiss or just Patty as he knew her. His jaw dropped. He took a knee.

"What? How? What's going on? You're

our passenger?" Normally cool as a Norwegian fjord, Gene was truly unnerved for the first time in his life. Patricia simply looked down meekly, then looked at Gene and raised her eyebrows in mock surprise. After her chance meeting and intimate dalliance with the young American flyer, she had surmised that he must be part of Freddie's crew since virtually every other flight crew member was out flying the day's mission. It was a complication, but nothing that couldn't be overcome.

The encounter did not go unnoticed by Fred, busy with Mother doing pre-flight checks. He knew Patty would be there, but how in the world did Sergeant Jordan know her? Unless.

Fred turned awkwardly and looked down and back. His eyes caught Sergeant Jordan's then shifted to Patty, her head turning to look at Fred. Darling Freddie. At that moment, he knew. He knew he wasn't the only member of this crew to have enjoyed the company of their VIP passenger. It left him shaken. Gene just sat on the deck, staring at the guest, still in disbelief. Maddy poked Fred in the arm.

"You alright there Captain?" Maddy knew he had to keep his pilot focused and didn't know or care what was going on behind him.

"Yeah, yeah, let's go. Let's finish up and get this bird in the air." Fred turned to the task of getting ready to fly the unwieldy bomber, checking the lump in his pants pocket for his lucky shrapnel piece. He'd need it today. The rest of the drama would have to wait.

The sun was gaining height on the eastern horizon now and the green flare from the control tower signaled the pilots to begin moving their aircraft into position on the taxiway. With the space of a bomber between each plane, nearly the entire taxiway was covered with B-24's as dozens of twelve-hundred horsepower open-exhaust engines created a thunderous noise. One plane after another moved into position for takeoff as the previous one lifted into the air. With the green light from the control trailer, each pilot released brakes and surged ahead, cautiously using most of the six-thousand-foot runway to ease his heavily laden bird into the morning air.

Fred resigned himself to the task. There was work to do and a very long day ahead of him and his crew. With no other choice he shrugged it off. Too much to worry about now; he'd find a chance to talk to Sergeant Jordan once they landed in Poltava and see exactly what the hell was going on.

# Chapter Twenty-Two

*Over Exposure* was among the last to get airborne, lifting stubbornly into the crisp October sky, working hard to gain altitude and join the rest of the squadron at the assembly point, formed up and anxious to head to Cologne. The bomb group had taken hell from intense flak yesterday with twenty aircraft damaged, and their presence over Cologne would be no surprise today either. Men in every plane inhaled deeply and girded themselves for a tough day in the air.

Looking back, Fred motioned to Sergeant Jordan to get back to his turret. It was a bit earlier than usual to take his position and he never needed to be told, so Gene was surprised at the rude thumb motion. He hadn't said anything to Patty and they sat there unable to speak anyway, with the overpowering noise of forty-eight hundred horsepower thundering in their ears. Given the ease of their encounter yesterday, could it be that she had also shown favor to his captain? He decided to worry about it later.

Gene hesitated a second or two. Patty made the small size insulated flying suit look cute. He felt a warm growing sensation that was absurdly out of place given the present circumstance. The captain's abrupt instruction brought him back down to earth, and he scrambled across the impossibly narrow catwalk between racks of bombs to his station.

Patty just sighed. She had gotten herself into a bit of a twist. Still, she was on a huge adventure, far removed from the playgrounds of Bath, doing something important for the prime minister himself! How marvelously exciting.

The absolute cold is what shocked her the most. Patricia Prentiss inherently knew that the air was cold at altitude but this bitterly cold? How on earth did these men tolerate it, much less fight off attacking German planes, endure tons of bursting flak, and drop their bombs on target? Just flying was scary; how much worse would it be if they were attacked? Every man seemed to take it with only the slightest trepidation. Maybe the confidence came with the experience of having flown so many missions. Maybe they had settled themselves with God. Either way, she immediately gained a new-found respect for each one of them and admired their absolute bravery.

"How cold did it get, Gene?" Now Henry Thomas was curious.

"Well, depending on how high we were flying it could get down to about minus thirty degrees or so."

"Really. Must have been hard to concentrate being so cold. How did you ever get used to it?"

"We didn't really. But we had a job to do

so we did it. It was cold but that's just the way it was. I'm still here, aren't I? Got all my fingers and toes." And another important appendage too, he thought. Gene chuckled softly to himself.

Flying Tail-end Charlie was no picnic. The Liberator was difficult enough to fly without dealing with the turbulence caused by aircraft further ahead in the formation. Each group in the box flew at different altitudes to minimize the prop wash but it was a constant struggle to stay on position. Today the group would approach Cologne from the northwest for the bomb run. As the formation crossed over into German airspace, Fred got on the in-plane interphone, being careful not to make his announcement across the inter-plane frequency. It was almost time.

"OK, listen up. Once we get to the IP, I'm going to put out some smoke on one and four, then drop down and back and then head north before turning east. We might take some flak but if there's no fighters, we should be OK. Keep your eyes open and call out if you see any."

Fred yelled at Gus to make sure their guest was sitting on a flak jacket and as near the armor plate as possible. He didn't want to lose her, either to the mission or to anything else. He felt for his lucky shrapnel piece and reassured, prepared to pull off their little trick.

The target area was a mixture of part to nearly complete overcast and so it was likely that bombs would be dropped by Pathfinder Force flares or maybe the group would seek the secondary target. Good. A little confusion would help *Over Exposure* make its departure that much easier. Up ahead, small black clouds began appearing directly in the path of the bombers. The flak barrage had begun and the brave men of the 392nd were flying directly into it, along with one important British guest.

Figuring the co-pilot would have to be in on the deception, Colonel Melkin had ordered his mechanics to connect the oiling devices one to the pilot's location and the other to the co-pilot, making the installation easier and faster. It only made sense.

"Maddy, the first nearby flak burst we get, I'm gonna start the smoke." Maddy just nodded. Fred squirmed in his seat to look back at Patty. She looked up with a thin smile. The adventure was already more than she had imagined and the faint whumping noises of the flak bursts were growing louder but she gave Fred a determined look anyway. Fred sighed and nodded to her. They were almost ready for the deception.

Within moments, the bombers were in the middle of it, intense flak bursts filling the sky with hot shards of metal, pieces of rock, anything the Germans could find to fill the shells with deadly shrapnel. The group had not yet arrived at the IP but was taking a steady barrage of

88mm *Fliegerabwehrkanone* shells from the heavily defended industrial area below.

The Germans deployed three flak batteries of eight guns each into groups under one command, situated in multiple rectangular formations that allowed guns fired in unison to create a concentrated box of bursting flak shells to bring down invading American and British bombers. That was the theory but in practice, it took several thousand flak shells to damage or shoot down one plane. In some places the German flak batteries stretched twenty kilometers deep, bringing extended misery and sometimes death to the brave bomber crews as they attacked high-value targets below.

A burst just above and ahead of *Over Exposure* shot pieces of shrapnel into the Liberator ahead of them with a couple of pieces piercing the left wing of their own plane. That was the one they were waiting for.

Fred prodded Maddy's arm. "Now!"

Fred and Maddy pulled hard on the d-shaped rings attached to the ends of long wire cables that were routed to the gadgets located at engines one and four. Immediately, the cleverly rigged slender pots began spewing small streams of motor oil on to the hot cylinders of the roaring engines. Pushed out by the steady pressure of a carbon dioxide cartridge running through a small regulator, the quart-sized containers of oil were intended to spew smoke for up to five minutes, enough time in theory, for the B-24 to pull away, descend and fly out of sight of the group. Observers would naturally assume the ship had been hit and disabled, and possibly lost. The ruse had begun.

Fred guided the bomber down and to the right in a gentle curving descent that quickly separated his plane from the formation. Tail gunners on the disappearing group watched for chutes to blossom from *Over Exposure*. None were seen or reported.

"Keep your eyes open for fighters."

Fred Forshay's interphone command was heard but hardly necessary as turret gunners Sergeants Jordan, Taggert and Withers and the waist gunners were already nervously scanning the sky for Messerschmitts. Up front, Lieutenants Roberts and Feinstein did the same, Roberts doubling as the nose gunner when needed in the absence of a permanent nose gunner for *Over Exposure*. Since Radioman Withers had also been trained as a gunner, and normally had little to do as a radioman, and because Gus Fletcher was not a very good shot anyways, Withers also served as the top turret gunner for *Over Exposure*. In a moment, Lieutenant Feinstein gave Fred the course for Poltava. Fred and Maddy looked at each other. "Here we go."

# Chapter Twenty-Three

Taking advantage of a steady forty miles per hour tailwind, *Over Exposure* made about two hundred seventy miles per hour over ground on the long run to Poltava. Some thirteen hundred miles away to the east, it was well within the B-24's range of about twenty-four hundred miles, but still, the idea of flying over hostile territory for most of the way alone and unescorted gave the officers and crew of the solitary bomber a very real reason to be nervous.

George Feinstein's course as laid out in his mission briefing, kept *Over Exposure* away from major cities and their stout defenses, leading well south of Berlin, then on a great circle towards Kiev and on to Poltava, some four hours away. It was about noon in Poltava when they broke away from the bomber formation. Give another half-hour for the extra course maneuvering and they should be on approach to Poltava before 1700 hours local time. As the plane regained altitude heading east, Fred ordered the unnecessary bombs released above a large lake east of Dortmund, giving Patty a first-hand witness to the roaring airflow of the open bomb bay, adding to the exhilaration of the already exciting and dangerous events of the day.

Flying close to the ship's operating ceiling

at twenty-five thousand feet, Fred took advantage of the mercurial jet stream to make the best time at the expense of everyone's discomfort in the minus-thirty degrees frigid air. The sometimes unreliable electrically heated flight suits helped ward off the worst of the cold air but exposed skin was at risk. Gus made sure their passenger was properly connected to oxygen and was made as comfortable as possible.

George fed the course changes to Fred as the Liberator skirted along between Berlin and Leipzig through the less populated areas of central Germany, then commenced their direct global route as they crossed the Oder River north of the small town of Lebus. Unchallenged thus far, Fred felt a slight sense of relief. Even though they were still over German-controlled territory with several more hours to go, they had cleared the major industrial centers unscathed by attacks from the ground or the air. So far, so good.

Henry Thomas got up to stretch. It was noontime and Gene Jordan's fellow residents at the assisted living facility were shuffling their way to the dining hall, a parade of grey-haired men and mostly women passed in formation, on their way to one of the highlights of an otherwise boring day. An aide stepped in the card room.

"You wanna eat in here Mr. Jordan?"

Gene looked at Henry Thomas who just nodded. Why not?

"Yes, can you bring us two soup and sandwich orders?"

The aide looked at the visitor with mild contempt, as if sparing a lunch would be some major policy violation. Muttering to herself, she waddled off to the kitchen.

"So, were you in the ball turret the whole time?" Henry Thomas wondered how anyone could stay in such a confined, cold space for such a long time.

"Oh, yes," affirmed Gene Jordan. "We thought we'd get jumped by fighters at any moment being all alone out there. They had radar, you know."

Gene closed his eyes and could clearly see German fighters slashing into their formation, guns and cannons blazing, trying to kill him and his friends. He heard his fellow crew mates call out the positions of the fighters, their voices rising and falling in volume and anxiety with the rhythm of the battle.

"But no one came after you?"

"No, I didn't say that."

A different aide walked in carrying two lunch trays and put them down. A half-Rueben sandwich on rye and a small cup of Matzo ball soup on both plates, plus a salad garnished with cherry tomatoes and red onion slices.

"You want a soda?" The sing-song voice was both demanding and inquisitive but somehow friendly at the same time.

Gene and Henry Thomas both nodded. The young woman reached into her apron pocket and pulled out two Publix brand colas, put them on the card table and walked away. Both men tested the soup first and then began working on the sandwiches. Henry Thomas dabbed his mouth with a paper napkin.

"So, what happened?"

Oberfeldwebel Hans Ruhl of the famed Jagdgeschwader 51 fighter squadron was ferrying a battle-scarred Focke-Wulf 190 to the Luftwaffe repair facility at Graudenz in Poland, roughly along a route that would coincidentally intercept *Over Exposure* on its way to Ukraine. Since fighting gallantly at Normandy and with a history of scoring thousands of enemy kills, JG-51 had been forced back further and further into the homeland by the advancing Allies.

Alongside and slightly behind was his friend and cousin Oberfeld Franz Werner, also bringing a worn FW-190A for urgent upgrades. Both planes were in need of the R8 kits on their fighters to add protective armor for the engine and pilot and new, 30-millimeter MK-108 cannons enabling them to have more firepower when attacking the high-flying American bombers. Gene Jordan spotted the pair of German fighters approaching *Over Exposure* and called them out.

"Two fighters, 4 o'clock low. Looks like 190's."

Poor visibility from the flight deck was a design flaw of the B-24 and it was impossible for Maddy to look down and back from his co-pilot seat.

"I see 'em," added right waist gunner Sergeant Dick Talbot. "They're crossing underneath us."

Hans Ruhl noticed the lone bomber as the pair of fighters approached but held course for a few moments. The bomber crew would think he hadn't seen them. He hand-signaled to Franz, looking up through the canopy. Franz nodded, visualizing a flaming B-24 falling to the ground, girding himself for the attack.

Though carrying only the ammunition left from a prior ground support mission, Hans Ruhl knew they had to attack the straying bomber, wherever it was going. What it was doing alone heading east was not his concern. He wanted to claim kill number forty as a badge of honor. It would be a difficult chore with only a few second's worth of MG-151 20-millimeter rounds available. It would be better with the new 30-mm cannon rounds but it would have to do. He'd aim for the vulnerable bomb bay where fumes from the notoriously leaky B-24 fuel tanks were likely to be ignited – if the pilot had the bomb bay doors fully closed with the vapors trapped inside.

"Where are they? Where <u>are</u> they!" Fred called out on the interphone.

"I see them," responded Gene Jordan. He'd followed their flight, quickly pivoting the turret as the two fighters passed below. "Ten o'clock, low." Gene reached down near his feet to pull up sharply on the gun charging handles. The FW's would probably pass them, turn left and climb at the lone B-24 to attack from below, then turn and fly down for a second run. He'd seen it before and the maneuver, especially done against a single plane could be quite effective since only one set of guns from the bomber could be brought to bear when approaching from below or above. In a group formation, many guns from many bombers could target the marauding fighters but here, *Over Exposure* was on its own.

As expected, Hans Ruhl and his wingman went into a sharp left climbing turn, barely a speck in the sky, and the two FW-190s prepared to shoot at the underbelly of the B-24. The BMW-801 engines pulled hard, helped by the nitrous-oxide engine boost giving the FW's greater ability to attack at high altitudes. Gene Jordan called out what he saw. He briefly thought about Patty hoping she was sitting tight on the flak vest, not that it would help much against a German 20-millimeter cannon round.

"Here they come! Seven o'clock low!"

The FW's burned off some forward speed

154

in the climb towards the American bomber, giving both pilots perhaps an extra half-second of effective firing time as the closing speed dropped a bit. At five hundred yards out, Hans Ruhl fired and Franz fired with him. They both got off two-second bursts before veering away, catching return fire from Gene Jordan, Rob Lowry the left waist gunner, and Sergeant Withers in the top turret as the planes passed level and above the B-24. Smoke and flames burst from the engine cowling of the trailing 190, piloted by Franz Werner.

"Got one," commented Lowry, as calmly as if he had just hooked another fish on a Sunday lake outing instead of scoring a hit on an attacking fighter. In all likelihood, the hit belonged to the ball turret gunner who had a longer burst on the .50 caliber guns.

"Stay on them," replied Fred sternly, "They'll turn and dive on us."

The 190's had scored a few hits in the fuselage of the bomber, missing any vital controls and failing to ignite any fumes. Still, it had been terrifying for Patty, now hugging her flak vest for dear life and cowering close to the bulkhead of the flight deck.

Sergeant Withers scanned the sky above looking for the diving fighters, bracing for the deadly attack and expecting to see the flashing cannons at any second. They did not come.

"They've turned away!" Lieutenant Roberts spotted the two planes veering back to their original course from his position in the nose of the B-24, smoke trailing one of the fighters. Fred patted the hunk of lucky shrapnel in his pocket, taking a deep breath and glancing over at Mother who returned the glance with grin.

Franz Werner had been grazed on his right arm by one of the bullets from the American plane and the engine was smoking. The fighter plane was losing power and it was hard to see through the smoke although the sturdy BMW engine kept going. Hans was not about to risk his cousin's life any more than necessary in the wounded FW-190. Besides that, he might only have a few shells left to fire. Discretion in the face of a low ammunition count made sense. He waved Franz back to their course towards Graudenz. Better to make it to the base alive and get the planes upgraded than to risk his cousin dying for a single B-24. He'd get his fortieth kill some other day. When they got to Graudenz, he'd report the straying American bomber and let some map-reading officer worry about it.

Sergeant Jordan took a deep breath from his oxygen mask and let out a long sigh. His ears rung from the clattering of the .50 caliber guns mounted next to his head. He wished for a cigarette to calm his nerves. Maybe later.

The short battle over, Gus Fletcher stepped

back to check on their passenger. Patty's eyes were wide in fear but still she had a confident look about her. He gave her an "OK" sign and she smiled back at him. He reached between the pilot seats patting Fred on the shoulder nodding back behind him, indicating that the passenger was alright. Fred sighed and tapped the shrapnel piece. Hopefully that would be the end of the excitement on this trip. But he was wrong.

# Chapter Twenty-Four

General Rostislav Kaminsky was growing more impatient as summer turned to fall. The assignment to oversee the Soviet contingent of Operation Frantic as it was called was at first challenging and complimentary to his status as a great Soviet aviator, but now, after he had already captured the coveted Norden bombsight plus a few other secrets, and after the operation had slowly ground almost to a halt, he was ready to move on to something grander. There was much work to do in defeating the rapidly declining Luftwaffe, and in further developing the Soviet's own fledging fleet of bombers. Why had Stalin not recalled him?

A steady stream of usually unwilling female Russian nurses and administrative workers did little to soothe his temperament. In fact, he'd even slowed down with his conquests of these women to a once weekly encounter, and those had begun to hold less interest. The sex provided relief but the violence he'd lusted for previously no longer found any measure of satisfaction. It had to be the fact that he was now a forgotten hero, an aviation expert who was being left behind as his comrades drove to the west, pushing back the hated Germans on every front, killing German pilots by the score.

His disinterest in the nearly idle command at Poltava, as well as the little used fields at Mirgorod and Pyriatyn led him to relinquish order and discipline to his subordinates who, stuck in the same quagmire, were not particularly diligent in overseeing their men. His anti-aircraft gunners in fact, felt free to shoot at any plane that approached the field, American or otherwise. Fortunately for the visiting airmen, the aim of their Russian partners was poor. While some damage was suffered, there were no injuries other than to pride. The practice continued despite vicious protests from the American command staff.

On the ground, the remaining American support forces, significantly smaller now than at peak deployment, with little else to do played baseball and crafted a makeshift basketball court from unused runway sections, challenging their Russian counterparts to games that they consistently lost to the more skilled western visitors. Fights frequently broke out on and off the court and ball field, especially when a small group of Russian soldiers found a lone American at some remote part of the base. Punishment was doled out with abandon but the westerner's hands were tied.

The American soldiers were ordered to avoid retaliation as the senior staff as well as the very architects of Operation Frantic wanted to preserve friendly relations at all costs. They still were interested in proving the value of the operation in spite of the fact that most German targets of interest were well within range of attacks based in Italy, and a base in Siberia was still on the table for the continuing fight against the Japanese empire. The restraint only added to the problem, with some of the Russians taking it as a sign of total weakness by the visitors.

The last Operation Frantic mission had taken place a few weeks ago and a month before that, there had been a big uproar in the west when Josef Stalin refused to allow the Americans to fly relief missions to the Polish underground forces in the Warsaw Uprising. It was one of the nails in the coffin of the operation, and unleashed a measure of distrust between the Americans and Soviets that would soon mushroom even further.

On the 19th of September, the American 8th Air Force launched one hundred B-17's and more than sixty P-51 fighter escorts from fields in England to drop relief supplies to the Poles in defiance of Stalin's objections, landing at the bases in Ukraine. Only twenty percent of the supplies actually reached the struggling fighters and several planes were lost. Stalin was outraged anyway. By proxy, General Kaminsky was outraged as well. It was to be the last official mission of Operation Frantic as designed. The wall that was growing between the Soviets and the Americans and by extension, the British grew faster and taller.

So, General Kaminsky wondered, why was the 8th Air Force flying in a lone bomber with a diplomatic visitor? Was it an attempt to soothe the strained relations with the allies? Why did they not fly a transport plane from Tehran? Why a British envoy and not an American? Something didn't smell right and the dispatch had only mentioned a cooperative visit to share the latest medical advances in treating soldiers with head wounds. What did that have to do with him? Their own infirmary was used for regional recovery cases, true, but he was an aviator, not a doctor. No, there must be some other reason for the sudden visit. He crumpled the dispatch in his hand and tossed it in the trash.

Pulling on a cigarette, he gazed out an open window, enjoying the early afternoon sunshine and cool breeze. The first chill in the air was felt only a week ago. Winter was not far away. In the far distance, he could see the Americans playing basketball, one team with shirts, and one team without. What a strange game, he thought. Not the sort of athletic competition that would ever catch on in the Soviet Union.

Across from the Russian administration building, about a third-mile down the other side of the makeshift runway, Colonel Steve Powell studied his own curious dispatch, announcing the arrival of a lone B-24 with a VIP guest. They had welcomed hundreds of B-17s to the field, and lost a good number during the Luftwaffe raid a few months earlier. Why a B-24? The whole thing seemed rather odd but not so unusual as to cause alarm. Putting the thought aside, he turned to his adjutant.

"Captain Stillman, I need you to arrange temporary quarters for a visiting B-24 crew, four officers and six enlisted, plus one guest. A female guest, it would appear."

"A B-24, sir? And a female guest?"

"Nothing wrong with your hearing, Captain. Looks like it's a quick turnaround, maybe a day or two, so have the plane refueled and checked out after they arrive."

"Yes sir, I'll make sure everything's taken care of." He turned and went straight to the task.

Powell wondered why the 8th Air Force would send a single B-24 with no escort all the way to Poltava, with a woman on board no less. Something about a diplomatic meeting but it still made no sense. They could sure use some diplomacy though, so perhaps this guest was supposed to try and put out a couple of fires with the Russians. It couldn't hurt.

"Sergeant." Captain Stillman addressed the senior NCO in charge of all the shitty little jobs that came up at Poltava. Sergeant Woodrow

Tallman did every job to the best of his ability, whether it was leading a team to dig latrines, repair runway sections, oversee refueling, or even to appear to treat his captain with respect.

Senior Master Sergeant Tallman held everyone who worked for him to the same standard he'd adopted since the first day of boot camp; every job is done right, every job is done on time, no questions asked. With that attitude, he'd risen quickly through the non-commissioned officer ranks, and was one of the most senior black NCO's in the theater. Any resentment felt by his white counterparts or senior officers rolled off him like water off a duck's back. Their problem. He held a higher standard, like his pastor taught him.

"We have visitors coming in, just one plane, a B-24."

"A B-24, sir?" Tallman was a bit confused but quickly recovered. "I'll have it refueled and checked out soon as they come in, sir. How long will they be here?"

"Maybe two days. Get the crew a place to sleep. Four officers, six enlisted, and uh, a female guest, as well."

"Now, where..." Tallman caught himself before asking a dumb question. "I'll take care of it, Captain."

A female guest, huh? Tallman called out to his assistant, a white E-6 named Rourke.

"Find me a place for a woman to stay."

"Excuse me? You mean a new nurse?" Rourke looked at Tallman like he was looking at a misbehaving child, dispensing with any military protocol, as it might hint at him having some measure of respect for his black boss, which he most certainly did not.

"No, some kind of VIP visitor. See if you can rig up something private and out of the way. But yeah, you can put her with the nurses. An officer type I'd imagine."

"You got it." Rourke sat back down at his desk, going back to the task he'd just started before he was rudely interrupted.

"Today. Now!" Tallman's irritation was evident and even if he had a few hours to make the arrangements, he wanted it done now. That little prick Rourke could shove it if he didn't like it. Rourke and his other bigoted buddies, too, though fair to say, they weren't all that way.

Sergeant Tallman's rule of thirds applied in this situation, like it did to so many other things. The way he figured it, about a third of the white men had a real problem with him, a third seemed to be on the fence about his ethnicity, and the remaining third appeared to be completely colorblind. With that knowledge as his guidepost, he responded in kind and gained a fair amount of insight into human behavior in the process.

Like his pastor said, it wasn't all that

complicated. You treat others the way you'd like to be treated and love the Lord your God with all your heart and with all your soul and with all your strength and with all your mind. So far as he was concerned, that was enough. The rest would take care of itself. It gave him a constant peace of mind that was evident to anyone who knew him, and a sense of calm confidence that was confusing to anyone who tried but failed to get a rise out of the tough sergeant.

# Chapter Twenty-Five

Henry Thomas checked his watch. It was half-past two and he needed to check with Dolores at the store.

"I am quite fascinated by the story, Gene, but I need to call Dolores at the store to see if anything's going on. Would you like to take a quick break?"

"Absolutely. I have to visit the boy's room anyway. Help me get up."

Henry Thomas took Gene's arm, again noting the muscle tone the old man still possessed, and watched him amble away to the first-floor restroom. Dolores told him it was quiet, with less than a dozen sales, so not to worry, and she'd close up. Good. It would give Henry Thomas enough time to spend the rest of the afternoon with Gene.

"Look what I got!" Gene Jordan grinned, proudly showed off two coaster-size chocolate chip cookies he'd swiped from the cafeteria, placing one in front of Henry Thomas.

"So, where was I?"

"Flying into Poltava after the attack by the German fighters.

"Oh, yeah. Hell of a thing. I'm pretty sure I shot one of them down but it couldn't be proved. Old Lowry said it was him but he only had the one gun and I had two."

At Graudenz, Hans Ruhl flew slightly above and behind his wingman as his injured cousin gingerly touched down in the battered and smoking Focke-Wulf, then looked on in horror as the plane's left wheel collapsed, sending it into a wild cartwheel, bouncing once off the ground, then twisting up and curling upside down, landing with a sickening thud on the hard ground.

Straining to see behind him now and fighting back tears, Hans accelerated and swung up and to the right so he could make his approach and landing. Visions of their boyhood swam in front of his eyes – the fishing, the colorful kites they'd made, going on their first dates together with sisters they'd met at a nearby farm. All the memories flooded by in the moments it took to square up on the runway. By the time he rolled to a stop and opened the canopy on the 190, his cousin's plane had exploded and was engulfed in flames. Franz never had a chance. The Americans had killed him, and quietly enraged, he vowed to find that bomber and destroy it. The question was where could it be?

On *Over Exposure*, Lieutenant George Feinstein carefully calculated their position over strange territory. The orders had been pretty strict. The Soviets had little tolerance for allied planes that flew outside of the assigned corridor, above or below the permitted altitude, and definitely if they were ahead of or behind the posted schedule.

"Skip, we're over Soviet territory now," George called up to Fred. "We'll be there in about forty minutes."

"Roger that." Fred was tired of sitting and flying. The Liberator was sturdy enough but could be a beast to fly. All the B-24 pilots had large forearms, a testimony to the strength needed to muscle the big plane where they needed it to go. Sixty-seven feet long with a wingspan of one hundred ten feet, the plane could weigh as much as sixty thousand pounds at maximum takeoff weight. Loaded with eight thousand pounds of bombs, up to ten crewmen, machine guns, ammunition and fuel, it was a lot of plane to push around.

He thought of his crew, and of Patricia, too. They must be aching from holding their positions for so long, especially the turret gunners. Feeling as if they were free of any threats now, he called out on the interphone to have them stand down from the turrets and take a stretch. The most cramped of them all, Gene Jordan didn't have to be told twice.

It was decent enough of the skipper to let him come up from the ball turret when they were in heavy flak and no threat of enemy fighters on other missions. He truly appreciated that even though it may not have been by the book. For that, he held his captain in high esteem.

*Over Exposure* descended according to the flight plan for approach into Poltava. The expanse of red, yellow, and gold foliage framed the fields below in the last colors of the year before the leaves fell, leaving only the brown tree branches. It was quite a sight and reminded Freddie of leisurely autumn drives in western Connecticut into the Berkshires. His moment of reverie ended quickly as his training and experience brought the pilot back into focus. No need for oxygen now or the heating coils in the flight suits, although it was still cold.

They crossed the Dnieper River well south of Kiev at an unmistakably narrow section. Poltava was about eighty miles due east. The base had a single east-west runway with a parallel taxiway, with a series of one, two, and three story buildings housing the administration offices, mechanic shops and the infirmary. With the prevailing wind coming from the west, *Over Exposure* would have to pass the base, and then make a final approach from the east to land into the wind.

The main cluster of revetments was located at the northwest end of the runway, each section shielded by high earthen walls, with several barracks buildings and workshop areas located a few hundred feet away. Clustered together, the effect was less than ideal but it would have to do at the makeshift base. The entire field was surrounded by a series of trenches where airmen could take cover in case of an attack. During the June bombing by the Luftwaffe, the Americans found safety in those trenches as their Soviet counterparts attempted to put out fires, disarm Butterfly bombs, and of course, steal several Norden bombsights from the damaged B-17s all the while German bombs were falling and fires raging.

General Kaminsky's office was in the main building about midway down the main runway, a few thousand feet from the American's encampment and the Russian infirmary flanked the main building a bit farther to the east. Truck-mounted anti-aircraft guns were placed around the base perimeter or moved into position as needed and consisted only of machine guns. The base security had always been a sore spot for the American commander and during the June attack, the machine guns proved useless against the marauding German bombers, in fact serving only to frame the field in flashes of gunfire, making it even easier for the enemy to hone in on the base. It was like shooting ducks in a barrel for the attacking bombers.

At the other end of the field, a few additional revetments capable of holding another twenty or so bombers occupied a spot on the southeast corner of the taxiway and a group of tents and Quonset huts were erected at the distant southwest corner, serving as additional living quarters for the American mechanics and security personnel with a section cordoned off for the nurses. *Over Exposure* would land towards the west, and pull into the unoccupied revetment area at the west end of the base. If they made it through the Soviet defenses.

Lieutenant Roberts saw it the flashes of gunfire first.

"Skip, why are we being shot at?" Tracers arced up towards the lumbering B-24 as Fred passed the base to make his turn to the west.

"Crap. Navigator, we're on time, aren't we?" Fred didn't want to get shot out of the sky now, especially not by Russian allies.

George Feinstein checked his calculations carefully. "Yes, we're here when we're supposed to be, I'm sure of it."

"Damn. They should know we're coming, right?" Fred continued east and made the turn to land. Maybe the Russians didn't recognize their B-24, having mostly seen the distinctive B-17 over the last few months.

"Hang on. We're taking it in."

The crew took their usual spots for landing, including Gene Jordan who plopped down near Sergeant Joseph Withers, next to

Patty, as close as he could, drawing her flak jacket around her.

"They must have recognized us now, Skip," said Roberts. "I think they stopped firing."

Fred just shook his head. Damned Russians. "I thought they were our friends."

"We're going to be OK!" Gene shouted above the din as the plane bounced and bumped on their final approach.

"Nothin' to worry about!" Patty mimicked the phrase she had heard Fred say several times, confidently smiling at Gene and holding on to his arm as they touched down.

The B-24 rolled to a stop near the west end of the strangely constructed steel mesh runway and was then directed to the first one of two taxiways nearest the barracks buildings, to a large turnaround space adjacent to the fuel bunkers. Following the ground crew, Fred turned the Liberator around to face the taxiway and cut engines. Safe and sound, just like he'd promised Patty. Now what?

# Chapter Twenty-Six

Hans Ruhl was both furious and heartbroken. He walked slowly past his beloved cousin's burning plane, all attempts to reach the pilot rendered impossible by the intense heat. Franz was gone. What would he say to his aunt, that he had killed Franz by trying to shoot down an American bomber when he should have continued his ferrying mission? What would she say to him? How could he defend his blood lust for making another kill when it cost the life of his favorite cousin?

Reaching the administration building, Hans increased his gait. He burst into the operations room demanding to see someone in authority. By no means a senior rank himself, at the moment he cared nothing for chain of command. He wanted to know where that bomber was going and how he could find it.

"Yes Oberfeldwebel, I am sorry for the loss of your wingman. Accidents happen." The flight sergeant was clearly outranked by the officer speaking to him but was not deterred.

"We saw and attacked an American B-24 bomber heading to the southeast not long ago. I must know where it was going."

Duty officer Hauptmann Karl Schreiner was not impressed.

"I presume you acted on orders to attack the bomber?" Flight Sergeant Ruhl hesitated.

"We had ammunition; it was flying alone with no cover. It was our duty to attack."

"I see. And your wingman was killed in the process."

"He's... he was my cousin." Now the gravity of what happened started to sink in. Hans sat down, suddenly weary.

The German captain let the man sit even though he had not given permission. He took a seat next to the grieving flight sergeant.

"Sergeant, look up." Hans slowly raised his head, heaving a sigh. "There are three American airfields in Soviet territory, in Ukraine about nine-hundred kilometers to the southeast. That could be the only place they were headed."

Hans looked at the captain with a blank stare, unable to process the strange information.

"We bombed their main base at Poltava several months ago and destroyed seventy of their B-17s. It was a stunning victory. I am told there have been some missions back and forth to these bases over the summer but it is quiet now."

Hans just stared straight ahead. His cousin was dead. The men who killed him were many miles away. There was a hole in his heart he knew nothing could fill.

"Come, have some coffee. We will service your plane overnight and you can return to your unit. I will make it a priority. The installation of the armor is simple and the cannons can be swapped out quickly. I'll have you back in the air within twenty-four hours, hum?"

The sooner the captain got this troublesome flight sergeant off his base, the better he would feel. No need to have an interloper making a scene here, not when morale was so poor already.

Hans Ruhl took the coffee and a sandwich as an aide directed him to a temporary barracks and a dry cot. He quietly ate his sandwich, not because he was hungry but because he knew he needed the energy for tomorrow, when he would hunt down the B-24. The problem that occupied his thoughts as he eventually drifted off to sleep was how to fly nine-hundred kilometers deep into Soviet territory with a plane that only had a fuel range of eight-hundred kilometers.

Fitfully asleep, Hans suddenly bolted upright, leapt from the cot and raced back to the operations room.

"Herr Hauptmann!" Hans interrupted the captain who was looking over a stack of maintenance records. He looked up and sighed.

"Yes, sergeant, how may I help you?"

"Sir, would it be possible for your men to mount two drop tanks on the wings of my plane?"

The captain thought for a moment. Hans

knew that too much thinking would not be a good thing.

"Sir, I barely made it here with the fuel I had. With the added weight of the armor plating, I think it would be wise to have extra fuel for my return trip."

"Yes, that's fine," and dismissed the flight sergeant with a wave of his hand, knowing full well that he had just been lied to. No matter. He had dozens of other worries to occupy his time.

Hans returned to his cot. The extra six-hundred liters of fuel would give him enough flight time to find that B-24, and destroy it, on the ground or in the air. Preferably in the air so the enemy would crash and burn just like his beloved cousin. If the bomber had flown to Poltava, then so would he.

# Chapter Twenty-Seven

It wasn't much, but the hot meal hit the spot, as the Yanks liked to say, and the small room that had been crafted for her was at least dry and as comfortable as one could expect. It would do.

"Miss Prentiss." Colonel Steve Powell spoke from outside the small space she'd been assigned, even though it was divided from the space around it only by a series of blankets hung from spans of rope.

"Yes." She stood up and weaved her way around the small corridor that had been assembled to give her a bit of privacy. It felt good to be in regular clothes after hours in the itchy flight suit.

"Miss Prentiss, I'm Colonel Powell. The general would like to meet you."

So soon. Well, there was no time to waste anyway. She needed to turn on the charm and find a way to get into his office. No better time than the present.

It was evening now, and dark other than the low lights that lined a path from the west end of the runway to the administration building, several hundred yards to the east. They walked in silence, the colonel preferring to know only what he was told, to escort the British visitor as needed, and to otherwise stay out of the way. A lighted doorway at the front of the three-story building shone more brightly that one would expect in war time, even though the front lines were hundreds of kilometers to the west.

Standing outside was a tall, rather handsome man, his jacket off in spite of the slight chill, a rather informal looking figure with a full moustache and combed back hair. Without the military jacket, he could have been anyone, but Patricia knew he was the general. The general who beat and raped women. He beamed a wide, fake smile as she approached.

Taking the cue Patricia slowed her pace a bit and eyed the man from head to toe, making sure he could see her gaze as it stopped somewhere near his belt line. This did not go unnoticed by the general and he stood a bit taller as she approached him, holding out her hand in greeting.

"General, this is Miss Patricia Prentiss, the British hospital administrator from St. Hugh's and the special envoy we discussed earlier."

The general took her hand gently, surprisingly so, and bowed slightly in greeting.

"Welcome to Poltava," he offered in Russian with a thick accent. "It is an unusual pleasure to have you visit our small facility."

"Thank you, general, uh..." She replied in the man's native language as naturally as if she'd spoken it for years, which she had.

"Kaminsky. Rostislav Kaminsky at your service." The general clicked his heels together like proper gentlemen might do, although he was nothing of the sort.

"Well, you've had a long day I am quite sure but we have business to discuss, yes?"

Colonel Powell looked on, oblivious to what was being said.

"Yes we do. I hope we can be of service to your hospital staff. We have developed some very successful techniques in treating head wounds and..."

"Yes, we can talk about all that tomorrow after you've had some rest. Will you come see me for a late breakfast in my office?"

It was almost too easy. "Yes, of course, I'll come back at 9 a.m. if you wish. I will need about three hours to completely explain our findings and then I'd like to talk with some of your medical staff if I may."

"Yes, I will give you the entire afternoon if that is what you wish. Perhaps you will stay a few days with us?" The general raised his head slightly in anticipation of her answer. "By the way, your Russian is very good, even the accent."

He was pouring it on thick, hoping to find a way to get a little more out of this attractive British spy before he had to kill her. Hospital administrator... did the British really think a Hero of the Soviet Union could be so gullible?

"We can take as much time as you wish," she replied, "But for now, I think I will retire."

"Until tomorrow morning, then."

"Good night."

Colonel Powell escorted Patty back to the tented camp, watching the shadows for any lurking Russian soldiers, feeling his hip for his service automatic. They would not think twice about having their way with a pretty woman, no matter the consequences. Patty walked briskly, wondering just how dangerous a man this general was, and if she could dominate him as she had so many other supposedly influential men. The morning would tell the tale.

Henry Thomas shifted in his chair a bit. It was a typical padded folding chair that offered comfort for perhaps an hour at a time.

"So what happened with the pilot after you landed?"

"Oh, well, we taxied to a stop and I helped Miss Prentiss from the plane through the bomb bay. It was kind of an awkward situation but there it was."

The crew of *Over Exposure* was greeted by Captain Stillman who had orders to escort the female passenger directly to her quarters while Sergeant Tallman assisted the crew.

"Sergeant," Fred said, "I prefer if we can all stay together. We may need to make a rather rapid departure from what I'm told."

"Not a problem, Lieutenant. Just give me five minutes to change my arrangements a bit."

Fred asked his ball turret gunner to take a walk with him. They strolled along the sunny side of the plane, casually checking for any damage as they walked. Fred pointed out some damage not two feet away from Gene's turret.

"Sergeant, let me be blunt about something. When we boarded the plane back at the base it seemed to me you recognized our passenger. Is that so?"

Sergeant Jordan didn't know exactly what the captain had in mind but elected to be transparent with his reply.

"I did recognize her, Captain."

"Since this mission is secret, how is it that you recognized her?" His question had a dual purpose, first to see if anything was up between the two and second, to see if there had been any loose talk before the mission.

"Well, sir... after the mission was scrubbed yesterday, I took Spencer out for a walk and bumped into this woman who said she liked dogs and we started talking a bit."

"Yes, go on."

"Well, she was very friendly, if you know what I mean and well, one thing led to another."

"I see." He pursed his lips and folded his hands behind his back, a clear sign that he was upset. Fred's blood was curdling but he said nothing of it to his sergeant. "Was there any discussion of this mission?" He had to carry out the second part of his interrogation.

"No, Captain, nothing like that. In fact, I was pretty damned shocked to see her sitting in the plane this morning. I hope I didn't cause any trouble."

"Don't worry about it; it's just one of those things." Fred turned on his heel and strode away to find the black sergeant.

"So he found out you two had spent the day together. In bed." Henry Thomas was now leaning forward in his chair.

"Yeah, and I could see he was pissed off, and I knew right there that he'd been with her, too. Probably more than once. Boy was his face red as a beet. I can still see it."

"So what happened then?"

Fred didn't know what to feel. Angry, betrayed, hurt. But what of it? She had come on to him the same way not that long ago. Who else had she been with? Colonel Reed? Colonel Melkin? Fred sighed deeply. Whatever happened, they still had a mission to accomplish and it was only halfway complete. It was just as well that Patty had been escorted away. He didn't want to see her face at the moment.

# Chapter Twenty-Eight

Hans Ruhl was awake at 0600, not just because the cot he'd been assigned was no more comfortable than the cement floor, but he was anxious to see about his plane. He planned his new mission and it was simple. Find a map in the operations room that showed Ukraine, pick out a landmark that would take him to Poltava and find that bomber. If he had to ditch on the way back, so be it. Secretly, he hoped to make it back to safety after killing the American bomber crew so he could at least say to his aunt that he avenged the loss of her only son.

By 0700 the operations room was busy and the flight sergeant stuck his head in looking for the captain he'd spoken with yesterday. There he was, pouring a cup of coffee.

"Ah, flight sergeant!" He seemed pretty chipper for being assigned to this remote dump. "Come have some coffee and perhaps a roll."

Hans Ruhl nodded at the captain from across the wide but shallow room.

"Herr Hauptmann. Good morning, sir."

"Flight sergeant, I have some good news for you. I had my men affix the armor plating to the engine cowling and cockpit area last night. They did an excellent job and have just finished. Now, our armorers will replace your cannons with the newer 30-millimeter ones. You could be on your way well before lunch."

Hans was excited and grateful that the captain had given his plane such a high priority over others on the field. It was an honor.

"Thank you, Herr Hauptmann. Might I ask will I also be given ammunition for my return flight?"

"Yes, of course, and your wing tanks as you asked. We can't send you back to your base unarmed and without enough fuel. We will also load your machine guns. There were only a few rounds left in each. You really should be more attentive flight sergeant."

Had Hans known there were even a few rounds in the machine guns, he'd have used them on the American bomber yesterday. He let the mild admonishment roll off, nodding politely at the captain. What did it matter? That was yesterday and today he'd be equipped with the latest cannons, a full magazine of machine gun ammunition and even the newer armor plating. Success was assured. The only thing was to find the bomber.

Hans looked up from his coffee. "May I study your map table, sir? I want to make sure of my route back to my base."

"Yes, of course. Use this one over here, it shows the full theater both to the west and to the east." Hauptmann Schreiner knew exactly what the flight sergeant was up to and let it go. He probably would have done the same thing in the man's shoes.

Flight Sergeant Ruhl studied the map and quickly found a landmark he could not possibly miss – a painfully narrow stretch of the Dnieper River halfway between two larger reservoirs. It was due west of Poltava and the airfield itself was crossed by a nearby rail line running north to south. He'd simply fly at one hundred ten degrees from Graudenz to the Dnieper River and follow the river south past the U-shaped reservoir to the unmistakable narrows where it elbowed to the east and then he'd slingshot straight to the base. He couldn't miss Poltava if he tried. Now if only the B-24 he sought was there.

# Chapter Twenty-Nine

After an uneventful and uncomfortable night at Poltava, Fred found Patty at the mess tent getting coffee the next morning. She was radiant in her blue suit, looking a little overdressed for the location and the circumstances but better to be attired as formally as possible for what she was about to do. What *was* she doing?

"I see your suit didn't get wrinkled on our trip." Fred was his usual charming self.

"Oh, good morning." She almost spilled her cup. "Yes, considering I sat on my garment bag the entire way, I think I look pretty sharp."

Even here in the middle of Ukraine Patty was on point.

"So, what exactly is going on here? You're not really trading hospital tips and tricks are you?" It was more a statement than a question.

"I really can't say..." Patty took a step backwards.

"Look. I put my life and the lives of my men at risk to get you here. We even faked battle damage so we could carry out this little drama, and we nearly got shot down for our efforts. You owe it to me to come clean, about everything."

Patty motioned Fred to a table away from the coffee mess. They sat down as she took a sip of the bitter coffee. She sighed heavily.

"Look, Patty there are no colonels here now, just you and me. What gives?"

"I'm going to visit the Russian general and try to find out if he's gotten hold of the Norden bomb sight. Churchill himself needs to know. Beyond that, I don't know. I just need to get in his office and find out what I can."

Fred let out a low whistle. "OK. OK, I got it. You really are a spy."

"Well, don't say that too loud, Freddie." The charm was turned on, just like a light switch. Her comment disarmed him.

"So, how are you going to find out?"

She reached into her coat pocket. "I have a Mickey, isn't that what you call it? A drug to knock him out. Then I'll search his desk for the documents I need and we can leave."

It sounded so simple but nothing was simple in this war. The trick was how to get the general to take the drug and then leave as quickly as possible without rousing suspicion.

"Does the Colonel here know you're about to drug the Russian base commander? Don't you think that will cause a stir after we suddenly leave with the general passed out in his office?"

"He's been told that my presence here may cause a disruption." Disruption indeed, as if relations at Poltava weren't on the skids already.

"I don't know. Doesn't seem right to

whack a hornet's nest then run away and let someone else get stung."

"I'm told the embarrassment of being duped by a woman will prevent the general from taking any overt action. Something about his pridefulness." That was the plan, anyway.

Fred thought for a moment. "OK, so we're going to have to leave in a hurry, am I right?"

"I'm afraid so. I'm meeting with the general at 9 a.m. and I will go through my presentation about the wound care. That will take a while. I hope that he'll bring lunch in then I can drug his drink. After he's knocked out I'll search for ten minutes or so, that's all it should take, then I'll leave his office on my own."

Fred's tactical mind considered the situation and the layout of the airfield.

"It's about a half-mile from the building to our plane. It's going to take you too long to get back. Someone will find him; an orderly, a guard."

Fred's eyes rolled up. He was thinking. "I'll have someone stationed about halfway between us. He'll signal when you come out, and I'll have a jeep come pick the two of you up and we can skedaddle."

Such a funny word. "I hope you mean we can leave." Fred laughed.

"Yes, and look, take this with you." He handed Patty his lucky shrapnel piece.

"What's this?"

"It's what almost killed me but now it's my good luck charm. Take it with you. You're going to need it. Trust me, it works."

Patty pocketed the small metal ball and stood up. "See you after lunch."

# Chapter Thirty

Hans Ruhl rolled his newly refurbished FW-190A-R8 into position for takeoff. The Hauptmann had been true to his word. He was armed. He had two wings tanks of extra fuel. It was going to be a good day.

The FW pulled smartly into the air as the flight sergeant wrestled with the controls. With the added weight forward, the plane was a bit less responsive, needing a slightly heavier hand on the stick. It would take some getting used to, but knowing that he and his BMW engine were better protected made up for the inconvenience.

He cleared the perimeter of the base and turned southwest for five minutes, then swung around to his intended heading towards Ukraine. Towards the B-24 whose gunners had killed his cousin.

Fred pulled his crew together for a briefing. He wanted everyone alert.

"I can't tell you exactly why, but we're going to be leaving in a hurry today."

Blank faces stared back at him. So what else was new?

"Our passenger is here for a specific purpose, and once that purpose has been accomplished, we're leaving right away. Lieutenant Schweitzer, I want you sitting in your seat ready to get us airborne at a moment's notice. Station yourself there no later than 1100."

*Lieutenant* Schweitzer? We're being rather formal today. The crew looked at each other wondering what brought this on.

"Sergeant Fletcher, are we refueled and ready to leave?"

"Yes captain and I've already done a pre-flight so far as I can." Good old Gus, his baby was his first priority.

"OK, I want you in the plane with Maddy." Apparently we were back to being informal.

Now it was time to take advantage of the fact that Sergeant Jordan had a vested interest in the safety of Miss Prentiss.

"Sergeant Jordan, station yourself halfway between the revetment and the three-story administration building over there." Fred pointed out the ugly facade of the weathered brick edifice. "Keep staring at the front door until you see our guest leave. She'll be in a hurry. Wave both arms when you see her and we'll come pick you both up." Gene nodded.

"George, please find a jeep that works and sit in it over there near the mess tent and when you see Sergeant Jordan wave his arms, drive quickly up the taxiway to pick up our passenger. Sergeant Jordan, you begin running back towards the plane after you see the lieutenant drive your way. He'll pick you up on the way back."

"OK, Taggert, I want you, Lowry, Talbot, and Withers nearby and when we leave, get into your combat positions for takeoff."

"But cap, we don't usually..."

"I know. I'm not saying there's going to be shooting when we leave, but we just don't know. Get into your positions and ready your guns as we leave. Lieutenant Roberts, you too."

"Everybody got it?" Heads nodded. "OK, have something to eat, and stand by the plane. Jordan, head over to that cutout in the taxiway so you can see the admin building. You're on point."

"Got it, Captain. Captain, where are you gonna be?"

Fred sighed and pointed. "I'll be over there by the barracks buildings, so I can see everything. Maddy when you see Sergeant Jordan waving his arms, light up the engines."

Fred well knew that there was more to it than simply turning a switch to start engines but the point was well made. They were going to leave on very short notice.

Patricia Prentiss was nervous but didn't let it show. After all, she'd been around injury and death from this damned war for over four years. It toughened her, filled her with a resolve she'd never imagined she would possess. She was about to do a deed for her prime minister! Who would have imagined that back at St. Hugh's? She felt for the small vial of chloral hydrate in her coat pocket and the piece of shrapnel Freddie had given her. How sweet. The small SIS version of the Latvian Minox camera occupied her other coat pocket. Hopefully the light was good in the general's office. At midday, it would be as bright as it could be. Her small valise held the medical papers Colonel Melkin had dummied up for her presentation. She was ready, she hoped.

General Kaminsky was waiting outside the administration building in full uniform, including his coat and the gleaming Hero of the Soviet Union medals. How impressive a figure he made, standing tall. He had a ruddy complexion, and the confident appearance of an accomplished man. She smelled his virility and it excited the young British spy.

"Yes, good morning Miss Prentiss. Won't you come right in?" Her smile was a little too wide for such a formal visit. What else did she have in mind?

"Good morning, general. Thank you for taking time to see me."

"My pleasure. My pleasure, indeed."

Good. The general didn't like stairs. His office was on the first floor, on the left side of the entrance, across from the stairway. There was one guard by the front door of the building but no reception area, just a series of hallways and offices. The wood floor was worn and creaky. She'd have to remember not to run from his office later as it would make too much noise.

Eight hundred kilometers away, Flight Sergeant Ruhl of the German Luftwaffe was pointing his Focke-Wulf fighter into the mid-morning sun, heading towards the Dnieper River. With time to reflect on yesterday, his heart was heavy with the loss of his cousin, and for the knowledge that he'd been the reason behind it. Today was his chance for justice. What did it say in Deuteronomy 19:21? "Your eye shall not pity. It shall be life for life, eye for eye, tooth for tooth, hand for hand, foot for foot."

# Chapter Thirty-One

General Kaminsky's aide brought in a silver plated tray with slices of hearty, locally baked bread, eggs from a nearby farm and a pot of coffee. He placed the tray on a round table that doubled as the general's meeting table, not that he held a lot of meetings. It was more for show since all of his directives were given to subordinates standing at attention in front of his desk. Today however, he had a special guest. A British spy disguised as a hospital administrator. He was going to enjoy today thoroughly.

Patricia and General Kaminsky chatted in Russian as the general talked about his two Hero of the Soviet Union medals and the bust of him waiting in his hometown. Patricia listened intently, sipping the dark bitter coffee and nibbling on the bread. She had little appetite for the food but was anxious to get on with the other details at hand. Her mind drifted as the general droned on.

"And so, after flying for two hours in the fog and rain, I finally spotted the Panzer tank column ready to move into attack. I was almost out of fuel, but just made it back to base and reported the exact location after which our forces were able to mount a pre-emptive strike to disable the column. That was my first Order of

Lenin."

He was now explaining some of his other awards. What a self-centered egoist, but you had to be to survive in the Stalin government, and even then one served and survived at the whim of the dictator.

"Your breakfast – is it not good?"

"Oh it's fine general, I was just thinking ahead to my presentation. Whenever you are ready, I can begin."

"Yes, of course. Would you like my medical director now or perhaps later on this afternoon?"

"My first package is just for you general, and then I have some other details I can share with your medical staff later." What a lie. Melkin had only provided enough details to explain a rather vague, broad-based cooperative program designed to be convincing enough while also being exceedingly boring.

"If you can ask that we are not to be disturbed for the next couple of hours that would be useful as my material is quite detailed."

"Yes. Please prepare your materials and I will advise my adjutant."

Patricia opened her valise and took out several folders marked *Current Treatment Doctrine, Advances in Head Wound Protocol,* and *Implementation.* It looked convincing enough and was provided in both English and Russian.

"Yuri," General Kaminsky knocked on his adjutant's door. "If you don't hear from me in three hours, come interrupt us. Until then, I wish to be alone with my visitor." He raised his eyebrows for effect.

"Absolutely, General. Three hours." The adjutant nodded with a half-smile.

Patricia thought about dumping the chloral hydrate into the general's coffee but thought the better of it. Fred would not expect her so soon and it was unlikely the general was going to finish cold coffee. She'd have to wait for lunch or perhaps he'd make them both a drink after her presentation.

"Where were you while the meeting was going on?" Henry Thomas was trying to visualize the base layout.

"Well, halfway between the ship and the administration building was roughly in the middle of the runway and that would have looked pretty awkward. I stationed myself along the taxiway instead and Gus gave me a few tools so it looked like I was repairing something. It was better than standing there with my thumb up my ass, for sure."

General Kaminsky returned to his office, making sure not to drink any more coffee or eat any more of his breakfast. The lovely spy was not going to get the best of him so easily.

"So, where do we begin?" He took off his

uniform jacket. Patricia could not help but notice his ample biceps and strong physique. The general caught her looking.

"Yes, there is not much to do here for entertainment so I try to stay in shape."

Patricia caught herself blushing and quickly moved to open the first folder.

"General, if you want to bring your chair over here, it will be easier to see what I have."

Kaminsky sighed. Such language was quite forward and it was an unmistakable signal that she was interested. Good. It would make the conquest all the easier. He moved his chair as close as possible, so that his visitor could not help but brush against him while turning pages. He could smell her and she smelled very good. Dewy and a bit earthy. This was going to be a good morning.

George Feinstein borrowed a jeep from the base crew with no difficulty. There was little for them to do and the loan of an idle jeep to the visiting B-24 crew was no problem whatsoever. He parked the jeep as instructed with a clear view of the plane to his left, Fred at his 10 o'clock position, Sergeant Jordan at his 12 o'clock and the administration building at his 1 o'clock point of view. With no small amount of alarm, he noticed three Russian soldiers approach Sergeant Jordan in a dirty GAZ-67 utility vehicle. It was their version of the reliable Willys Jeep. He put his finger on the starter button just in case.

Word had been passed that the Russians were finding ways to pick fights with the Americans as relations continued to deteriorate at the base. The three soldiers jumped out and began questioning Jordan, gesturing with their arms, making motions towards *Over Exposure* and talking loudly, although George could not quite hear them.

Sergeant Jordan stood as tall as his frame would allow, only rising to the chin of the shortest Russian. They continued to gesture and badger the sergeant who was now distracted from watching the admin building.

Suddenly, the trio laughed and clapped, slapping the American flyer on his back. One of them shook his hand and they drove away towards the opposite end of the runway and their barracks. George sat back and relaxed a bit, wondering just what the hell had happened.

In the general's office, the briefing was proceeding as planned and Patricia Prentiss found a rhythm to her talk, making a convincing case even though the Russian didn't really hear a word of it. He was too busy noticing the cut of her clothes, wondering if she was as amply constructed up top as she appeared to be. A loose button on her blouse gave the general a generous view every time the spy bent over to flip the papers. He was feeling quite warm.

Patty paused a moment and reached into her coat. "Cigarette?"

"Why yes, thank you."

After a short break she moved to the second folder, explaining some of the latest treatment methods, which in fact were exactly what she had been working with back at St. Hugh's. For this part, there was no added emphasis or fakery required. She was quite adept and convincing. The general paid closer attention drawn by the rising passion in her voice as she spoke about faster recovery periods and dramatically reduced incidences of infections. The work was actually quite impressive and could be useful. He'd remember to keep the documentation after she suffered her unfortunate slip and fall, striking her head on the corner of his desk. It would be a very difficult moment and his adjutant would swear he witnessed the accident when the inquiry began. The general thought he'd even run outside the office to yell for help as a convincer.

Flying low and fast, Hans Ruhl piloted his Focke-Wulf with the newly installed armor and cannons into sight of the Dnieper River. He was approaching his objective. He turned right to follow the river, keeping well to the west of Kiev just in case, but within eyesight of the meandering waterway. Soon, he would reach the U-shaped reservoir and then the narrows where he would turn due east. He hoped and prayed that the B-24 with the big "S +" on the tail would be at Poltava.

At 1100 hours, Maddy and Gus climbed aboard *Over Exposure* after doing the five-minute external inspection. They ran through the routine as much as possible – hydraulic fluid levels, star valve, fuel selector valves OK; gas tank caps checked, flight controls checked, fuel valves checked, generators off. The remaining dozen or more checklist items would have to wait until they got the high sign, and then they'd have to hustle.

Henry Thomas got up to stretch. He and Gene took a walk outside to get a breath of fresh air. The afternoon was on the wane and Henry Thomas did not want to overstay his visit but so long as Mr. Jordan was willing to continue the story, he was willing to listen. In fact, the old man seemed to enjoy telling the seventy-year-old tale. They settled on a sofa in the entry hallway to continue.

"So, everyone was in position, the little scare with the Russian soldiers turned out to be nothing, and you were just waiting on Miss Prentiss to appear."

"We didn't know it at the time, but things were getting pretty interesting in the general's office."

"Miss Prentiss, you have been quite

thorough in your explanation of these new treatments and I can see where they will be very useful in treating our wounded. I appreciate the depth of your presentation on behalf of our soldiers who will benefit in the future."

She sensed a hanging thought on the part of the general. "But...?"

"But I think it is time to take a short break before we proceed to your final folder. Won't you sit with me on the couch for a few moments? I'll have our lunch brought in first and we won't have to be disturbed." He stuck his head out the doorway and barked a command for food and for them not to be disturbed until mid-afternoon. Moments later, sandwiches, a bottle of water and a bottle of vodka appeared. Perfect.

This was it. The general was going to move on her. He'd been peeking inside her blouse all morning, the one with the loose button she'd carefully arranged. He was getting impatient and frankly, so was she. A powerful man was for her, an overpowering aphrodisiac.

"I'm not particularly hungry general but a drink would be nice. My throat is rather parched after going over all the documentation." Patricia removed her suit jacket, palming the vial of chloral hydrate in a practiced move.

The general poured two glasses of vodka and handed one to Patricia. He sat open-legged on the couch and drank deeply, like a satisfied man after an honorable hard day's work in spite of the hour, setting his glass down on the end table. Patricia sipped some vodka and put her glass down as well. It was time.

The general patted the space next to him for her to sit. Patricia smiled coyly and shook her head, no. Instead, she straddled his waist, presenting her open blouse to the general's face. As the general lost himself in her cleavage, Patricia reached her arms behind his head, unscrewed the top of the small vial of chloral hydrate and emptied the contents into the general's glass.

# Chapter Thirty-Two

It was past noon and Fred was becoming anxious. He'd expected Patty to appear by now. Being on edge for a few hours was nothing new to the pilot of a B-24, but when a woman he cared about deeply was involved, and probably in harm's way, well, it was an extra strain that was difficult to bear.

Sergeant Jordan was beginning to feel even more conspicuous in his position on the taxiway. Someone was bound to take note before long but he kept his eyes on the administration building doorway. A very nice British woman who had recently made his intimate acquaintance was up to something he didn't like. If only he knew the rest of the story.

At 1240 hours the front door opened and Miss Prentiss stepped out, stopping to ask the guard to light her cigarette. Her hands were still shaking but she knew the innocent gesture would reduce any suspicions the guard might have about her leaving the building unescorted by the general. She smiled at the guard and thanked him in perfect Russian and casually but without dallying, began walking towards Gene who immediately waved to Fred and Lieutenant Feinstein. In a flash, the jeep was on its way to pick up Miss Prentiss first, and barely slowing to collect Sergeant Jordan, the three sped towards *Over Exposure*. At the same time, Fred sprinted back to the plane to complete the checklist that Gus and Maddy had already restarted, waving the remainder of the crew on board as he ran.

Inside, Gus and Maddy raced through the checklist – mainline and battery selectors, auxiliary power unit and hydraulic pump, brake pressure and parking brake, gyros. The list went on. Fred checked to see if Roberts had remembered to enlist the ground crew to remove chocks. There they were. The checklist continued. Automatic pilot off, superchargers off, props in high RPM. They could do it in their sleep.

George parked the jeep behind the tail of the Liberator and the three scrambled aboard through the bomb bay, the lieutenant and Patricia squeezing along the catwalk forward and Gene taking station near his turret. As soon as they got airborne, he'd go through his own precise routine to enter and engage the turret systems.

He desperately wanted to ask Patty what had happened, but there was no time. It was then he saw several dozen Russian soldiers running towards a truck depot at the far end of the runway. The depot where they kept among other things, truck-mounted machine guns. Something had happened. Something bad.

Looking out the canopy of his FW-190 with the R8 package installed, Hans Ruhl spotted the unmistakable U-shape of the reservoir fed by the Dnieper River and just south of it, the narrows where he saw the distinctive elbow bend that pointed his plane due east. Racing through the cool October air his only focus was to fulfill his completely unauthorized mission, one that if he survived, would probably result in his death by firing squad anyway. It didn't matter. Avenging his cousin was the only thought on his mind, atoning for the death that he had caused, and snatching a bit of honor to make his family proud in spite of his tragic mistake. It was only one hundred sixty kilometers now; he'd be at Poltava in fifteen minutes.

"Wait, so what happened between Miss Prentiss and the general?" Henry Thomas felt like pages had been ripped from the middle of a good book he was reading.

"I'll get to that. Don't you worry." The old man smiled within, knowing that his friend's jaw would drop when he revealed the rest of it.

"Let's go, we gotta get going!" Fred was confident but concerned at the same time. It was pretty damned obvious things had gone wrong with whatever Patty had been up to, and the Russian soldiers racing across the runway were a sure sign of trouble. "George. Where's the wind?"

"No wind, Cap. If anything, it's a couple miles per hour west to east."

It would have to do. No time to taxi to the other end of the runway. They were going to leave the revetment hot and go full power as soon as he could line up *Over Exposure* for takeoff.

They all heard it. The sound of an incoming mortar round. It exploded a couple of hundred yards away in an empty revetment and everyone now knew Miss Prentiss had stirred up a hornet's nest. It was time to go.

Screw the missing fire guard. Fred shouted "Clear!" to the ground crew, and by force of habit ran through the regular engine starting sequence – engine three, four, two and then one.

"Ignition switches all on! Throttles cracked!" Maddy was yelling. "Booster pump on!" The pace was frantic but professional, like surgeons plucked from a suburban hospital operating room and dropped into an emergency field tent behind the front lines.

Maddy and Fred started engines as quickly as they dared, being careful to do it in the absolute minimum time while getting their asses out of harm's way as soon as possible. There was no time to wait for the ideal oil temperature. They had to leave. Fortunately every engine meshed and none were flooded. They were good to go. Fred waved chocks removed and surged ahead. Another mortar round whumped nearby, also in a protective revetment. Good thing the

Russians were poor shots and presumably they had to avoid hitting the regular contingent of Americans but all bets were off at the moment. The security contingent for the American ground crew drew arms and prepared to repel the Russians. A nice October day had turned to hell in the twinkling of an eye.

The cylinder head temperature on all engines was inching toward 120 degrees. Fred prayed it would reach minimum temperature by the time they reached the runway. Maddy finished the checklist items as Fred held back pressure on the throttles and taxied with throttles alone only as a veteran B-24 pilot could. His palm rested on the throttle knobs and his finger tips curled over the throttles. Fred was a master violinist; *Over Exposure* was his finely tuned instrument.

Lieutenant Roberts called out on the interphone. "We've got company coming!" Four trucks appeared as dots in the distance, heading their way. Machine guns fired, spitting yellow bursts from the top of each truck. It was impossible to shoot straight on a moving truck rambling over a bouncy, metal-mesh runway and in any case, the Russian gunners were not very accurate even when the truck was parked. Still, it was unnerving even though they were nowhere near effective range. The mortar rounds stopped after the first two explosions. Someone had thought the better of possibly hitting the American ground crews. It was the plane they were after.

Fred called out on the interphone. "Withers, open fire on those trucks as soon as I initiate the takeoff run. Rob, you too." Lieutenant Roberts doubled as the nose turret gunner and was ready at his station. If he had to shoot at his Russian allies, so be it. After all, they were for some reason, shooting at him.

Since the Liberator had been on the ground less than twenty-four hours, Fred and Maddy skipped a full run-up, clearing engines instead while Maddy frantically scanned the instruments looking for any malfunctions, not that anything less than ideal would stop them now. Maddy closed the cowl flaps to trail, and called out "booster pumps on, auxiliary hydraulic pump and power unit off, generators on!" Maddy, Gus and Fred frantically finished the checklist, and were ready to roll. No time to waste as the Russian trucks were appearing larger and they could hear the gunfire now. A few rounds pinged off the metal deck beneath them as the ground crew who had been watching scrambled for cover.

Fred wrangled the Liberator into position and in spite of wanting to jam full power, he gradually increased power on all throttles exactly as he had learned so many months ago and done so many times since. The plane began to gain speed and soon, gained rudder control. Maddy flipped on the throttle friction locks as they reached the stops. They were at full power now. Fred called out on the interphone.

"Withers, Rob, clear the runway!"

Sergeant Withers in the top turret and Lieutenant Roberts in the nose turret began firing bursts of .50 caliber ammo straight down the runway at the approaching trucks, scattering them to the left and right. One toppled over as it hit the hard ground and on the other side, one truck collided with another, sending both into a spin. Withers and Roberts continued firing as Sergeant Taggert waited his turn in the rear turret. He'd never taken off while seated at his gun station and his added weight in the tail was a slight risk but as *Over Exposure* reached one hundred twenty-two miles per hour, it lifted itself off the runway past the gun trucks, pulling into the thick autumn air as Maddy, Fred and Gus watched the gauges for anything unusual and wondered if they'd forgotten anything.

Sergeant Taggert couldn't quite deflect his guns low enough to target the crashed trucks to dissuade them from any further firing but as the plane cleared the end of the runway, gunfire erupted from the perimeter emplacements, with tracers drawing closer to *Over Exposure* as Fred made a gradual turn to the northeast. Taggert returned fire, expertly striking several of the truck emplacements. A few rounds creased the fuselage but the Russian gunners failed to slow down the departing B-24. Fred remembered to breathe. So did Maddy. They looked at each other in wonder. What the hell had just happened?

"That was interesting," deadpanned Lieutenant Roberts. The waist gunners took up their stations as did Gene in the ball turret. There were a dozen or more steps just to lower the ball, much less get inside, then ease in gingerly, right foot first then left foot, attach the safety strap and dog down the hatch so it was securely closed. Flip the overhead toggle switches to fire up the turret and gun sight. Reach down to yank on the gun charging handles. He was ready.

It was all eyes on the sky now, looking for enemy, or perhaps even Russian allied fighters. Lieutenant Feinstein scrambled to his work table, figuring the route to Brussels leaving Patty alone with her flak jacket and parachute. She checked her pockets and felt the bulge of the small camera and Fred's lucky piece of shrapnel. Lucky indeed. It had come in handy.

# Chapter Thirty-Three

One of the Luftwaffe's brightest and most productive and decorated flight sergeants, Hans Ruhl took great pride in the precision with which he flew, first in the venerable ME-109 and then later the Focke-Wulf 190. He'd struggled with the handling of the earlier 190 models at high altitudes but the steady advances in both engine reliability and power, and constant improvements in armament had now made the 190 the preferred bomber killer. And he was in a bomber killing mood today.

As children he and Franz had made and flown their own balsa and crepe paper kites. He preferred a more complicated box kite design while Franz stuck with the tried and true simple cross design. It was the length and weight of the tail that made the kite perform and they'd have kite fights to see who the better kite pilot was. They enlisted together, completed flight training together and asked to serve together, for the Fatherland.

The patchwork of green and brown farmland below was strangely comforting to Hans even though he was flying alone and unauthorized over enemy territory. The scenery reminded him of his early days of flight training in the Focke-Wulf FW44 biplane, soaring over low fields and valleys not terribly different from the landscape below him today. Hans sighed deeply. In moments, he'd know if his mission was in vain or if he'd find glory in the midday sunshine.

"What happened in the general's office?" Henry Thomas' tone was pleading, demanding almost, that Gene tell him exactly what had happened to cause such a clamor at the Poltava base with Russians shooting at Americans.

"OK, I'll tell you, but I didn't find out all the details myself until years later." Henry Thomas gave the old war veteran a quizzical look but elected to simply let him proceed rather than waste any more time.

"Near as I can tell, Patty took advantage of the general's libido as much as he had imagined taking advantage of her. At least that's how it started."

With the chloral hydrate swimming in the last few sips of the general's vodka, all Patty needed to do was get him to drink it. She figured that riding him like an American cowgirl would make him thirsty. The general did not need any encouragement to remove his pants and Patty hiked up her skirt, and then dropped on him suddenly, taking in the general with a single downward thrust. He was generously proportioned which caused Patty to shudder in delight. She was not one who needed a lot of coaxing to achieve full release, and in a moment, she did just that, pulling Kaminsky's face to her as she gasped in a rapturous flood of pleasure. The danger of her situation only served to heighten her anticipation. She was not disappointed.

Her unrestricted release triggered the general's own as he threw his head back in a toe-curling moment. They were still breathing hard as Patty gave the general the squeeze. He moaned, all thoughts of harming this delightful British spy erased, at least for the time being. Like a big cat who toys with his prey before the final kill, there was more to this temptress that he had to sample. Her unfortunate accident could come later today, after he'd taken his guest for another ride, or perhaps, two. At the same time, Patty had "the vermin" where she wanted him, utterly under her spell and in her control. Men could be so easy.

Eventually Patty climbed off the general and brushed herself off a bit, straightening her skirt which was now quite mussed and buttoning one of her blouse buttons. He just sat there dull-eyed as if he'd just been drugged, not knowing that indeed, such would be the case momentarily.

Patty reached for her glass of vodka and handed the general his.

"A toast," she announced with a sly smile.

"To Soviet British relations." She laughed

like a schoolgirl at her own small joke while the disarmed general reached his glass and touched it against hers.

"To another round of intense... discussion!" General Kaminsky downed the rest of his vodka, savoring the sting of it on his palate. He reached for Patty's coat for a cigarette, but instead felt two hard lumps in the inner coat pockets. He looked at her and couldn't quite focus. One lump felt like a small camera, the other a round hard object. A puzzled look crossed his face as he tried to stand.

The general's heart began pounding and beating rapidly. His breathing slowed. He felt sick to his stomach. What had she done? Gripping the coat with Fred's lucky shrapnel, he lunged at Patty, flailing his arms to strike her, like he had struck other women who had first pleased him and then annoyed him with their presence.

The acute overdose of chloral hydrate was probably enough to kill some men but in reality, Melkin had merely wanted the general to quickly pass out and wake up hours later with a massive headache, wondering what the hell had just happened. As it turned out however, the event unfolded with much more ugliness than he'd hoped for.

Patty deftly sidestepped the general's sloppy lunge and kicked him in the ribs as she recalled her training. With that, the general dropped her coat and fell backwards, the side of his head striking the top corner of his massive wooden desk. Knocked out by the drug or the blow to his head; it didn't matter. Patty grabbed the small camera while she put on her coat and shoes, getting ready to make her escape. First though, she needed to find the proof Churchill wanted. She began rifling through the general's desk drawers. In a moment, she found a folder titled simply, "Zhukov." That had to be it. General Zhukov was Stalin's chief commander. She quickly sorted through the dispatches in the thick folder.

With several black and white photos paper-clipped to the attached report, the American's Norden bombsight was described in detail according to Kaminsky's own evaluation, including notes about how it connected to the plane's autopilot, information he had gleaned from the American flyers. The paperwork also indicated that three of the bombsights had been recovered intact following the Luftwaffe raid at Poltava and were included in the shipment to Zhukov. That was it. The Soviets did have the American's secret bombsight and they'd had it for several months already.

Patty angled the paperwork for maximum ambient light and snapped photos of each page of the report. She heard a low moan from the general but he again fell silent. No time to waste.

Her eye caught a black shroud covering a lumpy object in the corner. Could it be? Finishing her photos of documents containing details of other stolen secrets, she returned the generals folder marked "Zhukov" to the desk drawer where she'd found it and stepped over to the corner near the window. Lifting the black fabric, she discovered a device that looked like the ones in the photos. The bastard had kept one of the bombsights as a prize! Men. She checked the general for a pulse. It was weak and his breathing was slow and shallow. At least he wasn't dead. That wouldn't do for diplomatic relations. Not at all. She noticed his pants were still down. Might as well leave them that way. His staff would probably not be too surprised when they eventually found him.

As Hans Ruhl's Focke-Wulf was closing in quickly on Poltava, Fred Forshay and his crew were gaining altitude and turning west northwest. Moments before at Poltava, the orderly who had come to retrieve the lunch tray found the general sprawled out on the floor, his pants around his shoes. He raced to alert the adjutant who followed him to the general's office. Seeing the general out cold on the floor, the adjutant reached for the desk phone, sounding an alarm that alerted the perimeter defense force. He then called the security chief, Colonel Polotny and told him what happened to the general and the fact the British woman was gone. The American plane! He could hear the engines revving up for takeoff in the distance.

Colonel Polotny directed four gun squads to the arms depot and told them to stop the American B-24 from leaving the base at all costs. Moments later, he watched vainly as the plane lifted off with his gun trucks tangled and wrecked on the sides of the runway.

It was the one time he'd wished his general had listened to the American guests when it came to base security. He wished they had done more than simply installing a ring of nearly useless machine guns as the base's only defense. The decision could result in the colonel facing harsh discipline or worse for letting the American plane escape. It was now his fault, and he knew it. Damned Americans. This act could not go without punishment. What would General Zhukov have to say? Or even Josef Stalin. He shuddered to think about it.

# Chapter Thirty-Four

*Over Exposure* continued to climb into thinner, colder air. Fred called out for oxygen masks on as the plane passed eight thousand feet and gave Sergeant Jordan the job of doing oxygen checks every fifteen minutes. It was going to be a long ride to Brussels but they had escaped Poltava undamaged and so far, no Russian fighters had appeared to convince them to return. George barked out a course that led the B-24 on a heading over the expansive tobacco fields north of Kiev, then a reversal of their inbound great circle track, ultimately steering south of Cologne then on in to emergency landing strip fifty-six near Brussels. Nothing to it now but the flying.

Coming in to Poltava at five thousand feet altitude, the FW-190 with Hans Ruhl at the stick was running smoothly and strongly and thanks to the twin wing tanks, had arrived on scene with fuel to spare. Hans strained to see the airfield up ahead, the checkerboard of steel mesh panels giving away its identity from several miles away. As he approached, Hans spotted a series of revetments on the northwest end of the runway scattered in a pinwheel fashion, enough to house at least two dozen bombers. They were all empty. Machine gun tracers arced towards his plane as he cut sharply to the right, climbing away from the Russian machine gun bullets.

The perimeter of the airfield was ringed with truck-mounted machine gun emplacements but the aim of the Russian gunners was poor. Hans paralleled the runway looking for other signs on an American bomber. The revetments at the opposite end of the runway were empty, also. Had his hunch been incorrect? He thought a moment and drove his plane into a tight turn to the northwest. It had to have been there. There could be no argument. But where to find the plane in the huge Ukrainian sky?

Having not seen a sign of the B-24 on his way in from the Dnieper River, Hans elected to fly back on a west-northwesterly route. It could be the only logical path for the missing bomber.

Sergeant Taggert saw it first, a small black dot below and to the left of *Over Exposure* but closing quickly. The FW-190 had a top speed of at least one hundred miles per hour faster than the larger and heavier B-24. He called it out on the interphone.

"You sure it's a 190?" Fred found it hard to believe there would be a single German fighter plane this deep in enemy territory. Unless. No, it couldn't possibly be the surviving fighter from yesterday's encounter. Why on earth would the pilot seek out a random B-24 and curiously, how would he have known where to look. Something was FUBAR.

"Yeah, Skip, it's the Luftwaffe all right and he's heading our way."

"OK everyone. Call him out."

Sergeant Lowry cocked his Browning M2 as did Sergeant Talbot manning the waist guns. The gunners in the turrets pulled hard on the gun charging handles. Everyone was ready for the fight. Gus checked on Patty who was wrapped in a flak jacket. She smiled bravely. Gus smiled back confidently, as if he knew a secret.

Moments earlier, Hans Ruhl spotted the bomber as he scanned the sky above the canopy of his fighter. He approached near enough to spot the distinctive "S +" on the tail. Closing his eyes briefly and sighing deeply, Hans turned to take aim on the tail of the B-24 whose gunners had killed Franz. The first to die would be the gunner in the tail of the plane. To that he swore on his dead cousin.

He approached slightly above the B-24 from the rear, slowing a bit to permit a good three-second burst on his first pass. The tail and top turret guns on the bomber lit up, tracking his path. He could swear he heard a couple of bullets bounce off his new armor and it filled him with a sense of invincibility. Weaving to avoid the gunfire, Hans steadied up at about nine hundred yards out and opened fire, targeting the rear turret of the American plane.

After hearing Withers open up on the

approaching German, Fred counted to three and pushed the yoke forward, putting *Over Exposure* in a slight dive just as the German opened fire. The ammo flew harmlessly past the B-24 and the fighter veered off at the last second, pulling hard to the left. Withers and Lowry tracked his turn for a moment until the plane was out of effective range.

Hans decided to try a lateral approach to the pilot side of the B-24. It would expose him to more guns but he'd have a much bigger target that would be easier to track as it maneuvered. The tail gunner could wait. He approached from the 10 o'clock position to cross the bomber and rake the fuselage with machine gun bullets and 30-millimeter cannon fire. The American bomber was a sitting duck.

The B-24's guns opened up, including Lieutenant Roberts in the nose turret and Withers in the top turret. In a second or two, Hans would be at the ideal range and he would destroy the plane with one pass. As few as four good hits from the MK-108 *Maschinenkanone* could bring down the bomber but he had to get close, perhaps three hundred yards away before firing. His approach became a slow motion nightmare. American bullets tore into his Focke-Wulf but it held, for the moment. At last, he pressed the trigger for the 30-millimeter cannons. Nothing happened. There was no time for a second chance. He had to veer away, taking more hits from the Browning machine guns to the belly of his fighter.

Now, what? The German flight sergeant stood off from the bomber as Hans considered his next move. He tried the cannons again. No response. Had those idiots mounted the new guns and only given him a few rounds of ammo? He tested the machine guns. They worked. Keeping the bomber in sight, Hans had to make a decision – attack with only his machine guns and hope for a lucky hit, perhaps in the cockpit, or try another day. The latter choice was absurd. He'd never find this particular aircraft again.

On *Over Exposure*, the interphone was alive with chatter. Why did the 190 not fire at them? His guns must be jammed. He chickened out. They shot him. Hope lived, and then Withers called out.

"He's coming back, 10 o'clock high."

Hans Ruhl decided to try and kill the pilots. Then, everyone else would also probably die. It was his choice of last resort.

Gus checked on Patty again. She pursed her lips in a confident and brave grin. Good girl, that one. Patty gripped Fred's lucky shrapnel piece with all her might.

Flight Sergeant Ruhl closed in for the attack. He decided to pass slightly ahead of and above the B-24 this time, taking his chances with the nose turret gunner, probably a bombardier with poor shooting skills.

The Focke-Wulf closed faster this time, its pilot opening up the machine gun attack at maximum range, deftly adjusting for the bomber's futile and awkward maneuvers. The tracers tracked high, a few bullets striking the right wing of the bomber. Hans pushed the stick forward, aiming lower, for the cockpit. He had only a second remaining to fire again.

Red fluid splattered inside the canopy of the 190, Hans staring at his own blood smearing his uniform as he pulled up. He hadn't heard the shots and didn't feel any pain, but there was blood, his blood warmly running down his arm, and clouding his view through the canopy. It was impossible to determine how or where he had been hit. He was still alive though, flying his fighter.

Turning and holding parallel to the bomber, Hans Ruhl considered his options in the deadly chess game. After a moment, he felt the searing pain from his wound and felt slightly nauseous. He was probably losing a lot of blood. So this was it. He was going to die today and join his cousin.

Fred called out on the interphone to see if anyone was hit. No one was hit and Gus reported no systems damaged. They were lucky. The German pilot was either inept, unlucky, or both.

Sergeant Talbot watched the FW in the distance, stalking them out of machine gun range. What would he try now?

Hans attempted to breathe deeply but could not. His chest and right arm hurt terribly. He felt and heard a wheezing noise as he tried to breathe. His pulse was racing. All things considered, the only thing left to do was ram the bomber and they would all die together. He decided to pace the bomber from above and dive into it, smashing directly into the point where the wing met the fuselage. From his approach angle, it would be impossible to miss and indeed, only one set of Browning machine guns would draw aim on him. The die was cast.

"What's he doing?" Fred demanded an update.

"He's climbing above us, Skip." Withers saw him hovering a few thousand feet over the bomber, matching its speed.

An oil line of the BMW engine of Hans Ruhl's plane began to spew oil on the hot engine.

"He's smoking, Skip." Withers' voice was growing agitated. Then sadly, anticipating the German pilot's next move, "I think he's going to dive at us."

Fred knew they were dealing with a madman. "Or dive *into* us. Withers, shout when he's about a thousand yards out. Everyone, hang on."

Hans Ruhl nosed his Focke-Wulf down and slightly to the right. He'd approach the B-24 from a slight left angle, firing his machine guns as he approached. The only question was if he would pass out before completing his suicide attack.

"He's coming, Skip!" Withers tracked the incoming fighter from the top turret and began firing at maximum range. The 190 was closing fast.

"Maddy power back on one and two and we'll both go hard left rudder when I say 'now'." Maddy just nodded. The maneuver might kill them but it was their only chance; roll into the angle of attack, aim down and turn hard to the left.

Withers shouted into the interphone. "Now!" Fred repeated the call for Maddy.

Maddy idled back engines one and two, the torque of the two remaining engines running full power on the right wing snapping the Liberator in to a yawing motion to the left. Both pilots pushed hard left rudder and turned the yoke, forcing the plane into a greater turn as the left wing dropped and the plane rolled sharply. It could be the beginning of a disastrous and final dive but it was also the only escape from the charging Focke-Wulf.

Bleary-eyed and fighting the pain in his chest, the German flight sergeant opened fire at one thousand yards, bullets tearing into the right wing of the B-24. Then suddenly, his target veered left, as suddenly as a big bomber could anyway, and Hans tried to follow but with the fast closing speed and the decreasing angle, it was almost impossible. He continued firing. It was his last chance to down the plane that killed his cousin.

Sergeant Withers steadied himself in the top turret as the B-24 violently turned, doing his best to track the fighter, unloading bursts of .50 caliber ammo as the ship dove left. The new angle gave an opening shot at the fighter's cockpit. Withers did not hesitate and unloaded a burst into the canopy of the fighter just as the pilot made his last desperate maneuver towards the B-24.

Bullets from the FW-190 smashed through the flight deck of the B-24 as the fighter passed high and to the right of the bomber, and as it passed, the left wing tip of the fighter clipped the outer edge of the Liberator's right wing. The fighter cart wheeled in the air, and then settled into a wide death spiral. No parachute was seen.

Fred restored full power to engines one and two, glancing over at Maddy who was holding his left arm and grimacing in pain. Struggling mightily, Fred centered the rudder and slowly pulled the yoke back to the right. The falling Liberator was slow to respond. Perhaps the aileron on the right wing was damaged or gone. Fighting hard at the controls alone, Fred strained with all his might on the yoke and rudders but the plane continued to slip left, the collage of divided tracts of farmland slowly spinning below, growing larger with each passing moment.

# Chapter Thirty-Five

Colonel Melkin arrived at Wendling as the mid-afternoon sun warmed the air with the temperature hovering at sixty degrees Fahrenheit.

He walked up to Colonel Reed sitting on a bench near the operations hut. "Nice flying weather I should imagine."

Frankly, neither man knew if the mission would take one day at Poltava, two days, or more. They hoped for one, and that meant the earliest reasonable arrival time at Brussels for *Over Exposure* was approaching. The ground agent there reported no activity thus far. There was no mission today for the 392nd, so the crews were scattered on and off base while the mechanics from the Sub Depot worked continuously to repair the flak and other damage from the previous day's mission to Cologne. It had been a rough one, with two of the 392nd's planes forced to make emergency landings at Woodbridge.

"What do you think?" Melkin was probing his American counterpart for any sign of doubt.

Colonel Reed rubbed his hands together and tilted his head. "Forshay's a good man. He has a good crew. If anyone can pull it off, he can." A moment's pause. "What about the girl?"

"Miss Prentiss is one of the strongest women I know. Naturally smart, well educated, made tough by her experience at St. Hugh's. And she hates Adolf Hitler as much as anyone. Not too fond of the Russians either, from what I gathered. She'll do her job."

"Then we should have nothing to worry about." Both men laughed nervously. "When will we know something?" Colonel Reed needed the mission to go off as planned, not only to advance his career but to properly account for the plane and crew.

"Could be as early as," he paused checking his wristwatch, "As early as now, I suppose, if they were quick about it. Might be tomorrow. Frankly, if things go badly, we might never hear." With that cheerful note, the Colonel stood and faced Reed.

"I could use a drink right about now. How about you?"

Colonel Reed checked his watch. "Why not? A quick one, anyway." They took a jeep for a quick visit to the *King's Head*. Colin would open up for them.

Sergeant Gene Jordan watched the Focke-Wulf spiral down towards the cascading landscape beneath his ball turret. He hadn't scored a hit on the plane, but someone did – probably his buddy Sergeant Withers. At any rate, that particular Luftwaffe fighter would no longer bother them. What the fighter was doing so far east was a bit puzzling but the sergeant put it out of his mind. Hopefully the captain was going to get the big bomber straightened out, lest he and the rest of *Over Exposure's* crew and sweet Patty join their German foe as red spots on the ground.

"So, you were hanging underneath this big bomber, spinning towards the earth and there was nothing you could do." Henry Thomas was fascinated, his eyes wider than ever.

"It was pretty hard to get out of that turret in a spinning airplane, and I had a great view. I figured the captain would figure out something so I just held on and watched."

"Fascinating. Since you're sitting here, I know he was successful."

As engines one and two regained full power, the overwhelming torque of the two right wing engines was negated enough for Fred to wrestle the plane back to level flight, for the most part at least. Sergeant Talbot confirmed the right aileron was damaged from his vantage point in the right waist position. OK, they'd endured more harm than that in the past. If there were no more fighter attacks, and they could navigate back across Germany without being shot out of the sky by a flak barrage, then today might have a happy ending after all.

While Fred was busy restoring stable

flight, Gus got the first aid kit and grabbed Miss Prentiss too, to come to the aid of Maddy, who was not doing well at all. His breathing was labored and he was in shock but they had managed to quell the bleeding. What they didn't know was that a German bullet had passed into Maddy's chest, putting his life on a timer.

Fred called out on the interphone to check on further damage and everyone's status. No other injuries, no other meaningful damage. He asked George for the quickest way to Brussels.

"We're on the fastest route, Skip. About five more hours." Five hours. Would Maddy be better off parachuting into German hands and faster medical care? Could he even survive the descent? Should Fred land and surrender his entire crew for Maddy's sake? What would they think of a second-generation German fighting for the Americans? Wouldn't Patty be taken as a spy? They certainly couldn't go back to Poltava. He looked over at Maddy who was beginning to stabilize a bit and it was as if he was reading his pilot's mind. He nodded weakly and gestured forward with his right hand.

"Go. Keep going," he said weakly.

Fred nodded and sighed deeply. Brussels it was. If only Mother could hold on.

# Chapter Thirty-Six

The afternoon of October 16th wore on as *Over Exposure* droned westward across Germany, the lone bomber unmolested by fighters or flak. Patty kept watch on Maddy. He was feverish, even in the zero-degree air, but smiled now and then with mock confidence as she and Gus did their best to keep him conscious. Maddy's breathing was labored and shallow. Patty felt a weakening pulse. The landing at Brussels couldn't come too soon.

To explain the appearance of the lone B-24, the story for the folks on the ground at the emergency landing strip was that *Over Exposure* was participating in a small leaflet drop mission over the Netherlands along with several other B-24's and B-17's and experienced severe engine problems, forcing an emergency landing. The passenger was a member of the intelligence team overseeing the drop. Melkin's crew would improvise any other excuses they'd need on the spot depending on the condition of the plane and would doctor any reports to account for date and time issues. They were on the alert scanning the eastern sky for any sign of an unescorted B-24.

As dusk overcame Brussels, a single B-24 bomber descended through the gathering gloom on final approach to the emergency landing strip near the Belgian town. Engine number one did indeed fail on Fred thirty minutes earlier and he'd feathered the prop, gingerly adjusting the throttle on the remaining engines to remain stable and sustain air speed. Gene Jordan navigated across the bomb bay catwalk to sit with Patty for landing, joined by Lieutenants Roberts and Feinstein in the now crowded space. They had made it. Now what?

Fred considered firing a flare to alert for a wounded crew but decided the less attention drawn to them the better. The landing was smooth enough on the short runway and he guided the B-24 to a spot pointed out by Melkin's ground staff. The plane hit a rut and the nose gear collapsed; the victim of unseen battle damage. It was a jarring stop and should have elicited a screaming protest from Maddy but he was too weak to care.

The weary but relieved crew evacuated the plane with Gus and Patty helping Maddy, handing him down to the waiting arms of Sergeants Talbot, Lowry, and Jordan. Melkin's lead operative confirmed Patty was with them and safe and relayed the information for transmission to Melkin's aide at Wendling. He summoned a stretcher and vehicle for the injured co-pilot.

It wouldn't do for the crew to hole up for the night at a local safe house. Melkin's team had arranged for transfer to the nearest supply and evacuation field, about fifteen kilometers distant, where a waiting C-47 would ferry them back to Wendling. A medic on the plane would do what he could for Maddy on the short trip over the channel. The ride to the S&E base would further tax Maddy's survivability but it was a Hobson's choice if any. They had no other facility for the gravely injured man.

The crew clambered aboard a deuce and a half covered truck with a jeep escort. The trip to the S&E field was not long but nothing was guaranteed. Patty stayed with Maddy the whole time, holding his hand, smiling confidently as he grew weaker. His skin felt clammy; his eyes glazed over but he hung on, through his own determination and Patty's encouragement.

The S&E field had been busy with C-47's bringing in supplies and ammunition and returning to England with wounded soldiers and airmen. Melkin made sure one was still on the ground for the crew of *Over Exposure*. It was 2100 hours and Melkin and Reed were sitting in the operations hut drinking coffee when an aide brought Colonel Melkin a coded message. It was only three words: "RED SKY TONIGHT."

Melkin was ecstatic. "Red sky tonight! They've done it! The crew is in Belgium. I'll be damned."

Reed breathed a sigh of relief. He too, was

happy, but what if the young British spy hadn't gotten what she was after? What if the ploy had all been for naught? He would have some serious explaining to do, and he would anyway, but with nothing to show for it if she were empty-handed. He needed something to substantiate the risk he had taken. An award maybe and possibly a promotion waited, or on the flip side, dishonor at the least, if not imprisonment. It was all or nothing.

At 0115 hours on October 17th, just ninety minutes before crew briefings began for the third consecutive attack on Cologne, a single two-engine transport approached Wendling, the base gleaming below under the light of a full moon. The C-47 touched down gently and rolled to a stop. Having been alerted to the unexpected arrival by Colonel Reed, the base commander had been given just a few details of a secret mission that had occurred without his knowledge. Had the British colonel not been there to provide the greetings and assurances of Winston Churchill himself, he'd have tied Reed to a tree already. Instead, he dispatched an ambulance to meet the plane and alerted the infirmary. He vowed to ruin Reed's career while putting on appearances for the British SIS officer.

Ignoring Colonel Melkin's demand, Patricia jumped into the ambulance with Maddy and Gus. Before the colonel could protest further, the ambulance sped away, Maddy hanging on for life, the results of the secret mission riding along with him in Patty's jacket. No matter. Let her play Clara Barton. Yes, let her ride along with the injured pilot. In short order she'd be dispatched by the medical staff to a waiting area.

Fred grabbed a ride to the infirmary as well after getting permission and assurances from Colonel Reed. The rest of the crew was taken for immediate debriefing by the colonels. Their information would also be useful to the SIS officer's summary.

# Chapter Thirty-Seven

Henry Thomas let out a low whistle. "Wow. So they really hustled you back, huh? And right into interrogation."

"Well more like debriefing but yeah, there was no moss growing under Colonel Reed's feet. I guess he had a real urgent need to know what had happened."

"Well, what did you tell him?"

"We sat around half-asleep while our colonel and the British colonel talked to Lieutenant Roberts and Lieutenant Feinstein, then they had us come in one at a time."

"Did they ask you about Miss Prentiss?"

"No, not for any specific thing and I'm glad they didn't because there's no way I could have kept a straight face about it, having done what we did."

"So what did they want to know?" Henry Thomas was brimming with anticipation.

"Well for one thing they made damn sure about telling us to keep our yaps shut about the mission. Then they just asked about when we broke off formation, had anything happened on the way to Poltava, and what happened there on the ground. I told them I was the lookout for Patty when she left the building and told them about the fighter attack. They seemed pretty curious about that, with the German fighter being over Soviet territory and all."

"Oh. So nothing about what Miss Prentiss had done."

"Well, no. I mean I didn't know anything at the time anyway."

"So that reminds me; how did you find out all the details? How could you have possibly known the whole story?"

"You wanna go for a ride?"

Henry Thomas and Gene Jordan walked over to the main entrance and Gene handed Robert the Haitian doorman his cell phone.

"You want a ride, Mister Gene?"

"Yes, thank you, Robert."

Robert pressed the Uber app on Gene's smart phone and summoned his ride, requesting Mary, his regular driver. Ten minutes.

The two men sat on a long park bench under the portico, enjoying the late afternoon breeze. A distant thunderstorm rumbled some muted claps of thunder and the cool, outer bands of air brushed over the men as they sat silently waiting for Mary in her Nissan Rogue.

"Where are we going?" Henry Thomas had forgotten to ask.

"You'll see. Just be patient."

Mary arrived in a moment and got out to open the front door for Gene, giving him a brief hug in the process. She liked the old man. He treated her with respect and even at his age, exuded a virility she found attractive. Forty-nine years old herself, she was only a generation behind Gene and hoped she'd grow old gracefully as he had done. She said hello to Henry Thomas with a big smile as he let himself in the back seat behind Gene.

"So, where are we going?" Mary more or less knew the answer but played by the script.

"My favorite place."

Ten minutes later, Mary guided the car past a wide gate into a secluded field off the main highway near Loxahatchee Road just south on Nob Hill Road. Henry Thomas looked at the entrance sign and was confused.

Mary guided the car to a familiar spot along a low curb under the shade of an expansive black walnut tree. It was a serene place, with gentle breezes and barely any intrusive roadway noise. Mockingbirds chirped happy songs in the nearby trees. The gentle splashing noises of a nearby fountain added to the serenity of the setting. The storm that threatened earlier had passed well to the south and was gone.

Mary helped Gene out of the car and the three of them walked across the finely trimmed grass. Gene stumbled slightly, stubbing his toe on a bit of unkempt turf but Mary had his arm. Presently, they stopped. Henry Thomas stared at a carved granite block, about three and a half feet high and two feet wide. Fresh flowers adorned the base, looking as if they had just been placed there, or maybe yesterday. On the smooth face was engraved the outline of a B-24 aircraft along with an inscription.

*Patricia Prentiss Jordan*
*May 1918 – June 1998*
*An Adventurous Spirit Flies Here*

A wide grin slowly creased Henry Thomas' face as he looked over at Mary and Gene. Gene just nodded back at him, holding back a tear. Mary smiled warmly, as she did every time she drove Gene to visit his departed wife. She knew Patty quite well after more than two dozen trips to the cemetery along with all the wonderful stories Gene had told her over the past few months. She loved her job when it meant connecting with people like Gene and his wife. She'd never met the woman, but felt as if she were a good friend. If only all her passengers could be friends.

Henry laid his hand on the marker, smiling to himself as he understood the full circle in the life of this story. He looked at Gene and nodded his understanding. So that was the rest of it. Patty and Gene had somehow come together after the war and had become man and wife. What a remarkable story.

"Thank you for this, Gene. It was quite a story."

"Oh, there's more to tell but let's get back. They're having T-bone steak for dinner and I don't want to miss it. I'll have Mary drive me to the store in a couple of days and fill you in on the rest of the details.

Even better. Henry Thomas loved a good story, especially when there was a coda.

# Chapter Thirty-Eight

A week passed since Henry Thomas visited Gene Jordan at the assisted living facility in Deerfield Beach. He hoped nothing had happened to the old man. A few things were unclear to him. How had Gene and Patty gotten together after the mission? Why did the Russian soldiers who were harassing Gene on the taxiway suddenly change their taunting to laughter? Whatever happened to Maddy? What did Churchill do with the information Patty brought him?

The last part became clear and he didn't need Gene to tell him. A little research on his own showed that indeed, Churchill was gathering information about the Soviet's capabilities and intentions. He learned they had the Norden bombsight along with other highly classified technology, most of it stolen from the Americans. With that data in his pocket, he called his command staff together early in 1945 to prepare a war plan against the Soviet Union to begin almost immediately following the end of the war with Germany.

Operation Unthinkable it was called, and among other components, it included a plan to turn Germany into a wasteland, starving up to ten million German citizens to death, along with detailed battle plans to conquer the Soviets and put an end to Communism as it then existed. Churchill was bent on it, and wanted the first attacks to take place early in July.

His commanders were aghast. The Russians had a four-to-one advantage in troops and a two-to-one advantage in operational tanks. Their air power was growing more potent by the day, and they already held huge swaths of land across Eastern Europe thanks to Stalin's aggressive land-grab strategy.

None of Churchill's intentions came as a surprise to Josef Stalin. He already had wind of the British leader's aspirations. In fact, the stalling tactics used by Montgomery when securing captured German weapons and troops told him that Churchill was going to use one hundred thousand German soldiers as new allies against him. He would crush them a second time, along with the British and any other allies the prime minister might muster. The only worry was the Americans. Would they abandon Europe to bolster their fight against Japan or stay? Did they have the rumored atomic weapon?

Churchill's Chiefs of Staff Committee deemed the proposal hazardous and militarily unfeasible, the polite way of telling their boss that he was out of his mind. The news that leaked about Churchill's plans made Stalin furious and only served to cement his resolve. Incidents like the incursion at Poltava and the death of one of his favorite generals along with his fear of American technology, his hatred of capitalism, and his need for a secure western border all contributed to the increasing friction between the Soviet Union and the west.

In the months following the war, Stalin was aware that Truman too, hated him and he hated Truman right back. The Soviets strengthened their foothold across Eastern Europe. Although there was no fighting, there was plenty of tension. In a speech to the South Carolina House of Representatives in 1947, multimillionaire financier Bernard Baruch warned in a speech, "Let us not be deceived - we are today in the midst of a cold war." The phrase was coined, and the conflict was defined for the next forty years.

Ten days after they last spoke, Henry Thomas opened up the antique mall finding Gene Jordan patiently waiting on the park bench out front. It was a nice morning and Henry was excited to see his friend. They went inside. Henry Thomas had Gene sit in a comfortable red leather arm chair while he made a pot of coffee.

"I have a question," began Henry.

"I'll bet you have more than one question." Gene knew he'd be there all morning and so asked Mary to come get him at noon.

"Why did the Russian soldiers who were

harassing you on the taxiway suddenly stop bothering you?"

"Oh, that. They were making fun of my size using some of the broken English they learned from the Americans. I told them my whole family was short, which is true, and that my uncle's name was Leo and that he was a gymnast with the Moscow Circus and he knew the famous clown, Mikhail Rumyantsev, or as they knew him, Karandash."

"How in the world did you make up that story on the spot?"

"Oh, it wasn't a story. My uncle Leonid was indeed a gymnast and often talked about Karandash. The guy was a famous Russian clown and had a routine where he made fun of the German soldiers. The Russians loved it, so I used it." Gene nodded sharply to add emphasis.

"Well, what do you know? What else haven't you told me?" He handed Gene a cup of freshly brewed coffee.

Intuitively, Gene knew what Henry Thomas wanted to know: how he and Patty had come together. First though, he needed to sew up a few other loose ends such as what happened to the co-pilot.

Maddy lay on the operating table as two field surgeons worked on him, accompanied by a bevy of nurses. It was the middle of the night but they were wide awake, on a mission to save the pilot. It had been more than a dozen hours since the man received his wounds. He had lost a lot of blood and had a bullet lodged behind two fractured ribs. They could get the bullet but internal bleeding was a problem. Transfusions weren't enough. Maddy loosely gripped Fred's lucky shrapnel piece in his right hand. Patty gave it to him on the ride in the ambulance and told him not to let go.

At 0640 as twenty-four crews of the 392nd Bomb Group prepared to take off for Cologne for a third time, a small metal object fell to the operating room floor as Lieutenant Maddy Schweitzer gave up his life. The exhausted doctors found Patricia Prentiss and Fred Forshay waiting on hard metal chairs in the hallway. They were awake only due to the combined effects of adrenalin and worry. The surgeon looked first at Patty, then Fred and simply shook his head and held out the piece of shrapnel. After a moment, Fred took his lucky shrapnel and placed it in his coat pocket. He held Patty as she softy cried.

"So what happened to her?"

"Oh, they whisked her away later that morning to take her to London for a briefing with Churchill. Colonel Melkin interrogated her for half a day or so and made his own notes while the film she shot was developed. He added the photos of the Russian documents Patty had taken to his report and together they were brought to

10 Downing. Far as I know she never went back to Wendling."

"And what about Fred and you guys?"

"Well, we stood down for eight days while they rustled up a new co-pilot and found us a new ship. We called it *Maddy's Angels.* We had another five missions to fly you know."

The conversation paused for a few moments while the men sipped coffee. A few customers came in and waved hello to Henry Thomas. Gene continued.

"So, I'm sure you want to know how Patty and I got together."

"It crossed my mind." About two dozen times at least.

"Well, after the war, I took a job in New York as a machinist for a family-owned manufacturing company. We made specialty high speed drills and saw blades, that kind of thing. I worked in the shop and eventually got promoted to supervise the entire manufacturing floor. The funny thing is, we began making these real precision drills that used expensive end units made in Germany, and I ended up working with a guy who had been a soldier with the Wehrmacht and was a POW here in the United States in 1943 until the end of the war. We became pretty good friends, actually."

"What about Patty?"

"Yeah, I'm getting to that. So one day in

1955, I get a call from the front desk that I have a visitor. A lady visitor. Someone from England who wanted to buy our high-speed drills for some kind of dental lab consortium."

"Patty?"

"You got it. Patty. Well, you can just imagine. Something like that could not have been just a coincidence. It had to be fate. We hit it off pretty well and kept in touch after she went back to London. She ended up leaving her job after six months and came to be with me and we had a great life together. Moved to Florida in 1990 and she died eight years later from a heart attack, but we really enjoyed each other. Traveled quite a bit, had a couple of kids. And I owe it all to my old dog Spencer."

Dolores came by to ask if Henry would approve a discount on an antique wall clock. He told her to give the customer fifteen percent and waved her away.

"Oh, and if you're wondering, when she settled down with me, she settled down completely, if you know what I mean."

"Oh. OK. Well, that's uh, that's good to know. I'm very happy to know that."

"Did you ever have contact with Fred after the war?"

"No, I never did. Not sure exactly what became of him. I know he wanted to keep flying and I heard he went to work for Pan Am."

So, thought Henry Thomas, there it was. Neither of them had a clue how Fred Forshay's flight log and shrapnel piece had found its way to Henry Thomas' store and in the end it really didn't matter. Fate had its own way of putting a strange twist into things. It probably came in a box of stuff from an estate sale and may have been passed down one hand to another before that. He'd never know for sure but he was confident that it didn't come directly from the Forshay family. He hadn't bought from the estate of a military family for quite some time.

There was one more thing he had to show Gene. But first, he had a question.

"Gene, did you want to buy the flight log and shrapnel? I mean, I would give it to you, but do you want them?"

"No, that's OK. You keep them. It's our little secret now. I'd only leave it to you anyway and you'd have it back before too long."

"There's one more thing, Gene. Take a look at this."

Henry Thomas opened the flight log to the last five pages, showing the mission notes Fred had made so long ago.

"Look at the log entries for the last five missions." Henry Thomas handed the little book to Gene. He carefully read each of the last five pages and then with a frown on his face, started over again.

"So?" He didn't understand.

"Here look at them in order."

*Mission #31: October 25, 1944 to Neumunster, longitude 9° 55' E, latitude 54° 10' N. We bombed an airfield, Pathfinder Force. No flak. No fighters. Some rockets.*

*Mission #32: November 5, 1944 to Karlsruhe, longitude 8° 25' E, latitude 49° 0' N. Started engines at 0600. Bombed marshalling yards as secondary target. Moderate accurate flak. No fighters. Some rockets. P.F.F. General flak holes.*

*Mission #33: November 6, 1944 to Weser Canal, longitude 9° 8' E, latitude 52° 20' N. The main compass froze up enroute. Bombed Weser Canal at the spot where it crosses a river. No flak. No fighters. Moderate amount of rockets. P.F.F.*

*Mission #34: November 11, 1944 to Isottrop, longitude 7° 0' E, latitude 51° 30' N. Cold started engines. Long run up due to lay off. Bombed synthetic oil refinery in northern Ruhr. Heavy inaccurate flak. No fighters. P.F.F.*

*Mission #35: November 16, 1944 to Eschwieler, longitude 6° 20' E, latitude 50° 55' N. War over for this crew. Troop support. Bombed concentration of guns and troops ahead of our lines. Flak moderate and inaccurate. No fighters. Landed at an English base on account of bad weather.*

"I still don't get it." Gene Jordan had read the log book a number of times. He was familiar with the contents. He was intimately familiar with each of the missions. He looked over at Henry and shrugged his shoulders.

"I'm sure it's an amazing coincidence," Henry Thomas suggested. "Look at the first word in each of the last five mission descriptions, right after he writes the latitude and longitude.

Gene Jordan studied the missions once more, and then looked up at Henry Thomas, his mouth wide open in amazement. It couldn't be.

*We – Started – The – Cold – War.*

# Epilogue

General Rostislav Kaminsky never awoke from the "Mickey" he had been given by Patricia Prentiss combined with the blow to his head. In the end, he was the victim of his own plan to kill the British spy but in a moment of weakness, he let her get the best of him playing his own game. His officers feigned outrage and threatened the American contingent at Poltava but nothing ever came of it other than even more mutual mistrust. The rank and file Soviet soldiers were glad to see "the vermin" go. Many of them had lost friends in the Luftwaffe raid trying to put out fires, steal American technology and defuse Butterfly bombs because of Kaminsky. To the general they said good riddance. To save face, Stalin simply awarded General Kaminsky the third Hero of the Soviet Union posthumously for his continuing contributions to the Soviet Union and the entire Poltava spy affair was quietly swept under the Kremlin rug.

The families of Hans Ruhl and Franz Werner mourned their deaths without the benefit or comfort of having remains to pray over and bury. As a memorial, they commissioned a modest stone marker engraved with a box kite and a cross-shaped kite with the boys' names and the phrase, *Fliegen Zusammen*. The stone marker was embedded at the corner of a fenced-in pasture where the wind consistently blew down from a mountain range across and through the wide valley.

Colonel Reg Melkin disappeared into the bowels of the SIS for another fifteen years, working feverishly on Soviet intelligence gathering operations. He remained as a trusted advisor to three prime ministers including Winston Churchill before dying in a suspicious auto accident. The cause was never fully resolved. He was laid to rest with full military honors.

Colonel John Reed was censured for his renegade spy mission although a letter of appreciation was filed in his record from the office of Winston Churchill. He was asked to resign his commission and eventually was hired by a college fraternity brother at a major financial institution to be an operations director where he led the implementation of mainframe computer technology and in later years, developments that led to the first automated teller machines.

Freddie Forshay stayed on in England for a few months after completing thirty-five bombing missions. He volunteered to fly several night radar mapping flights for the 25th Bomb Group (Reconnaissance) in a British Mosquito twin-engine plane outfitted with the latest H2X radar set and also flew the Mosquito on several mail runs for the 392nd. The Mosquito was much more nimble and fun to fly than the cumbersome but reliable B-24 and after the horrors of fighting off flak and fighters, Fred's joy of flying was partially restored. He also volunteered to fly planeloads of fifty-five gallon drums of gasoline for Patton's tanks to advanced landing grounds established to support the fast-moving 3rd Army.

After the war, Fred flew for Pan American Airways flying Boeing 377's and Douglas DC-7's, later qualifying on and flying the Boeing 707 jetliner. Fred also remained in the U.S. Air Force Reserve attaining the rank of Colonel where he flew the B-47 bomber on several operational and training missions. Fred hung on with Pan Am through the financial crisis of the mid-1970's and continued at Pan Am as an instructor until 1981 when he passed away in his sleep from a massive heart attack. Fred did not live to see his sixtieth birthday but raised a family and left a legacy like the others, as a member of America's Greatest Generation. He was buried in his Air Force uniform in a hilly, tree-lined cemetery overlooking a peaceful lake.

Henry Thomas loved history and irony and he found both in the marvelous story told by Gene Jordan. The past found new life not only in the antique objects with which he surrounded himself but even better, in some of the fascinating people he met and the tales they told.

Among his personal collection of militaria Henry owned a few World War II items; an A-2 pilot's jacket, a few medals and assorted patches. To this collection he now added two unique war artifacts that held the key to a remarkable story known only to a very select group; a small oddly shaped piece of shrapnel and an old, unmarked flight log containing a stunning secret that was nearly lost to time.

Lt. Henry Holmes (left)

Mission #27   Oct. 15, 1944

Cologne - 7°-0'E  49°-57'N

BOMBED MARSHALING YARDS
HEAVY ACCURATE FLAK &
ROCKETS.  WE  HAD
#1 & #4 ENGINES
KNOCKED OUT. #2
& 4 GAS TANKS &
CROSS FEED KNOCKED
OUT. 2 CYLINDERS ON
#2 ENG. KNOCKED
OUT.  HAD QUITE A
TIME. COULDN'T USE
RADIO OR SHOOT

# About the Author

Mark T. Holmes is a commercial writer and former marketing executive. Following a layoff from a senior marketing job at one of the nation's largest credit unions during the past recession, Mr. Holmes formed his own Florida S-corporation, Idea Depot, Inc., and began writing high-end military transition and executive federal resumes, along with doing web development and optimization, plus writing marketing material for a message-on-hold company.

In 2014, Mr. Holmes released his first book, *Streams to Ford*, a book of poetry long in the making, followed in 2015 by *Always Ready – Coast Guard Sea Stories from the 1970's*. All books are available in print and Kindle format on Amazon.

Mark and his wife Sheri operate a retail location in an antique mall, and trade in antiques and vintage cameras. Learn more and see related photos online at www.artifactbook.com

Made in the USA
Middletown, DE
12 December 2018